OPERATION
ORCA
RESCUE

a Poppy McVie adventure

Titles by Kimberli A. Bindschatel

The Poppy McVie Series
Operation Tropical Affair
Operation Orca Rescue

The Fallen Shadows Trilogy
The Path to the Sun (Book One)

OPERATION ORCA RESCUE

KIMBERLI A. BINDSCHATEL

Turning Leaf · Traverse City, MI

Published by Turning Leaf Productions, LLC.
Traverse City, Michigan

www.PoppyMcVie.com
www.KimberliBindschatel.com

Print ISBN-13:9780996189033
Print ISBN-10:0996189033

This is a work of fiction. Names, characters, businesses, places, events and incidents are either the products of the author's imagination or used in a fictitious manner. Any resemblance to actual persons, living or dead, or actual events is purely coincidental.

Thank you for purchasing this book and supporting an indie author.

For my mom—
Thanks for taking me to the library to learn about
fireflies.
And for my dad—
Thanks for a childhood at the lake.

And to the brave men and women of the U.S.F.W.S. and their
counterparts around the globe who dedicate their lives to save
animals from harm. Their courage and
commitment is nothing short of inspiring.

May their efforts not be in vain.

The least I can do is speak out for those who cannot speak for themselves.

~Dr. Jane Goodall

OPERATION
ORCA
RESCUE

a Poppy McVie adventure

Chapter 1

Norway. Land of the midnight sun. Cascading waterfalls, deep fjords, breathtaking views and abundant wildlife—the mother lode to a notorious wildlife criminal.

Sure enough, a few weeks ago, Headquarters received an anonymous tip that Ray Goldman, the U.S. Fish & Wildlife Service's most-wanted, was sailing these waters, on the prowl for killer whales. Rumor was, he was planning a live-capture for the mega-aquarium industry. And I was going to catch him.

Special Agent Poppy McVie, reporting for duty.

Since U.S. law prohibits an American citizen from hunting, capturing, killing or even harassing a killer whale anywhere in the world, and we wanted him—we wanted him bad—here we were.

"I feel like a damn circus bear jumping through hoops," said Dalton as he ended the call with the informant. "I'm starting to think he's just some crackpot getting his kicks."

My partner, Special Agent Dalton, up until now, had patiently dealt with him through every stage, even promised the man that his anonymity was a top priority, but the guy still wouldn't even give his first name. We'd started referring to him as Johnny, as in: *Here's Johnny*, the nutjob.

"At least he stays on the phone longer than thirty-eight seconds now," I said. "Maybe Hollywood called and told him that even they'd given up on that old drama ploy."

"Hollywood." Dalton rolled his eyes. "I'm sure that's why he believes agents are all 'gun-wielding, cowboy cops who shoot first and ask questions later'." He paused, looked at me. "Well, maybe he's got you pegged."

"Hey!" I frowned. "We're making progress with him. Now we have a time and location to meet, right?"

"He said he'd be at the Vikinghjelm pub down on Bryggen wharf after lunch. I'm supposed to wear my sleeves rolled up and sit at the bar with a beer and wait."

"That's it?"

"That's it."

"All right. I'll go in ahead of you and scope out the place," I said, "see if I can identify him, then I'll keep an eye on him for any suspicious behavior before you arrive."

Dalton started shaking his head before I'd finished my sentence.

"What? You don't think I can handle a little reconnaissance."

"No, that's not it." The edge of his lip curved upward into a half grin as his eyes traveled down to my waist, then back up. A slight tilt to the head. "You don't exactly blend in."

"What? I blend in." I winked and, in my best Irish brogue, said, "Me Ireland's jist a 'op, skip an' a jump dare, fella."

"I don't mean your American accent, my dear."

I thrust my hands onto my hips. "What then? I don't *look* Irish enough with this red hair and freckles?"

"This isn't a tourist pub. It's a local hangout for dockworkers and fishermen."

"So," I said. "I can blend in."

He frowned.

Geez. "Have some faith."

I wasn't going to give this informant a chance to change his mind and slip out the back door. Ray Goldman was a ghost. If there was any chance, any chance at all, that Johnny-boy actually had real intel, I wanted a piece of it.

In the 1970s, Ray Goldman had single-handedly decimated the Pacific Ocean killer whale population. He had permits to capture, but so many died in his careless capture attempts, scientists say that group of whales might never make it back to sustainable numbers and have declared them endangered. During his escapades, some drowned entangled in the capture nets, some died after being tranquilized with darts, and in at least one instance, he and his cohorts feared the terrified orcas would capsize their boat and opened fire with high-powered weapons.

His rogue methods started a political shitstorm and details only emerged later, when his help finally talked. By then, he'd fled to Iceland, where, at the time, whaling was not only acceptable, but welcomed. Fishermen wanted the competition gone, claiming the whales depleted their stocks. Which is absolute bullshit.

In 1982, the International Whaling Commission enacted a total ban on whaling, trying to protect whales from total annihilation, but Icelandic whalers used a loophole to continue to kill whales on a commercial scale under the guise of scientific research. Like Japan still does today. Iceland only quit whaling because of a public boycott of Icelandic fish in Europe and the U.S., plus the threat of U.S. Government-imposed trade sanctions.

Even with the public outcry for the whales, Ray Goldman never showed an iota of remorse. Then, he simply vanished into the ether.

Until now. Assuming it's really him. But it seems plausible. China and Russia are building new mega-aquariums and the demand for live orcas has resurged. One live killer whale carries a one million dollar price tag. That's a lot of dollars floating around in the sea. And nothing brings a trafficker back to work faster.

I turned to head for the pub when Dalton's phone rang.

He held up one finger, signaling me to wait. "It's Nash."

Joe Nash was our supervisor, a legend in Special Ops. He'd been the Special Agent in Charge on my first assignment with Agent Dalton in Costa Rica. Dalton and I were undercover as a married couple, buying illegal animals for the pet industry. Nash thought Dalton and I made a good team. He had no clue that, before we caught the kingpin, we'd damn near killed each other.

Dalton punched the speaker button. "Yep."

"Hey," said Nash. "How's it going over there?"

"We're heading to meet the informant right now," said Dalton.

"Good. Proceed with caution."

Dalton flashed me a like-I-said look.

"I don't have to remind you, we're out on a limb on this one. I did some fancy dancing to get you on this special joint effort with NOAA. Your directive is to confirm it is indeed Ray Goldman, gather the evidence we need to convict, then call in the Norwegian authorities to make the arrest. Got it? Just do that cute couple routine and you'll slide in under his radar."

I tried not to roll my eyes. From day one, our fake marriage felt like it was headed for a fake divorce.

"Got it," said Dalton, winking at me.

"A lot of people around here have been wanting to bust this guy for years. Keep it by the book. I don't want any loophole he can slither out of."

"Right, boss," said Dalton and disconnected.

Before he could say anything, I said, "I'm going to head in."

He shook his head.

"What?" My cheeks flushed pink. "I'm quite sure I can handle a little reconnaissance. You just make sure you've got those shirtsleeves rolled up."

I turned on my heel and left him standing alone in the middle of the sidewalk holding onto his phone.

Bergen is the second-largest city in Norway, as modern as any other in the world, but for some reason Johnny-boy wanted to meet at the Bryggen wharf in Old Town.

A series of buildings lined up in a row, all the same shape and size, distinguished only by their bright colors—red, yellow, orange, and white. I wished I had time to explore, learn about the history of this place. All I knew was that these buildings had been here since the late Middle Ages, part of the Hanseatic merchant guild that stretched along the north European trade routes. There was even a Hanseatic museum here to get the whole, sordid scoop. Alas, maybe next time.

Occasionally an alley separated two buildings where a wooden-plank boardwalk provided passage to the many shops and pubs tucked behind the storefronts. On this late fall afternoon, the shadows were already darkening the corners. I made my way down the main thoroughfare, through the crowd of tourists, then turned down one of the deserted alleys.

When I managed to find the pub, I had to admit, Dalton had been right about it. The place smelled of stale beer and fish guts and everything was coated with the brownish hue of tar from decades of cigarette smoke.

Five locals hunched over the dimly-lit bar—fisherman, or dockworkers maybe. Two other men ate at a table in the corner. At another sat three looking like they'd spent the last ten weeks on a boat and had dragged themselves down the dock to land here before hitting the showers. Otherwise, the place was empty.

With the exception of the computer cash register, it felt like I'd stepped back in time to circa 1650.

Yeah, I got the looks, the side-glances, the what-the-hell-is-she-doing-here expressions. But hey, a girl should be able to get a beer in peace, right? Wouldn't take long and they'd forget I was even here.

I climbed onto a stool at the end of the bar and waited for the portly barkeep to mosey my way.

He wiped his hands on his apron—also appeared to be circa 1650 by the amount of crusty grime glommed onto the front of it—and gave me a curt nod, his way of welcome.

"A Beamish, please," I said in my best Irish accent. Everyone knows the Irish drink Beamish. None of that Guiness sludge.

In good time, a frothy mug of my favorite, tasty malt beverage was slid my way. I took a sip and settled in to watch for unusual behavior.

The five men at the bar eased back into their conversation. Thankfully, nearly everyone in Norway speaks English and I could follow along.

The one who sat on the end, closest to me, seemed to have the attention of the others and I got the sense he wasn't from around here. He was about my dad's age, though this man's manners would never have been accepted at my mom's table. He had both elbows propped on the bar, his chin leaning on grubby hands. His features—large, bulbous eyes, pointy nose, protruding ears, pencil-thin lips—weren't all that odd, individually, but the combination somehow didn't quite go together, like he was a toddler's Mr. Potato Head creation, come to life. Even his weathered skin resembled an old spud.

"I tell you what," he said to the other four men. "Another go at it?"

They glanced around at each other, nodding, then dug some paper kroner from their pockets and slapped them on the bar.

"All right," the first man said. "I'm a slippery fish in a cloudy sea; Neither hook nor spear will capture me; With your hand you must hunt and seize this fish; To see that it ends up in the dish."

The four fishermen's eyes darted about, to the ceiling, to the floor. One scratched his beard in thought. A few glugs of beer, some barstool shifting, but no one spoke a word.

"Not even a guess?" the riddler asked. He waited. "Do you need a hint?"

One of the men eyed the pile of cash on the bar and grimaced, shaking his head in frustrated resignation.

The first man slapped his hand over the money and slowly dragged it in.

"A bar of soap," I said, then quickly drew in my breath. *Dammit.* I'd said it out loud.

The man flashed me a dirty look.

I flashed back an innocent, apologetic smile.

He turned back to the men. "One more? Just for fun?"

A young, rosy-cheeked man with a round, cheerful face piped up. "Sure, man."

The riddler glanced at the bartender and some unspoken signal passed between them.

"What has rivers but no water, forests but no trees, and cities but no buildings?"

More head scratching and lip chewing. "Dunno," said the one on the far end, a young, blond man of about my age, built like a barn. He tipped up his mug and chugged.

"Me neither," said the bearded man next to him, shaking his head. "What's the lady say?"

All eyes turned my way. *Crap.* I was supposed to blend in.

The riddler glowered at me.

"C'mon. Nothin's ridin' on it," one of them said.

The riddler raised his eyebrows and nodded his consent.

Rivers but no water, forests but no trees. "A map?"

The men snickered and grinned.

"Put the lady's beer on my tab," the riddler said to the bartender. "Okay, boys. Another bet?"

The bearded man shook his head right away, but the guy next to him dug into his wallet, then nudged the bearded guy, goading him until he finally dropped a bill on the bar. "My money's on her," he said, his gnarled finger pointed my way.

I shook my head and turned my attention to the contents of my mug. *Why didn't I find some hidey-hole in the corner with a view of the bar and keep my big mouth shut? Dammit, McVie. Blend in. Blend IN.*

The others nodded their agreement and coughed up the cash.

"Fine by me," the hustler said. He leaned forward on the bar as though ready to tell a ghost tale of old 'round the campfire. "I can't hear you, but I can touch you; You can feel me, but you can't see me; I can't see you, but I can kill you; You can't kill me, but you can hear me."

The blond barn on the far end dropped his face in his hands, then shook his head, tipped back his mug, and drained the contents in one gulp. The others seemed to try to solve the riddle, their eyes glassy and tired.

The bearded man raised his finger. "What about it, sweetheart?"

Crap. I couldn't win either way. If I didn't answer, the four men would be in an uproar. If I did, the hustler would get pissed off. I gritted my teeth. *I hate hustlers.* "The wind," I said.

The bearded man flung his head back and roared with laughter.

The hustler didn't flinch. He saw his opportunity. "Double or nothing," he said.

The men shelled out the cash without hesitation.

"No, no," I said, shaking my head. "I'm not—this isn't…"

"All on the girl," the hustler said, his potato-face puckered with amusement.

I kept shaking my head, no, but the men were back in the game now.

They pushed the cash into a tidy pile.

With a starchy grin, the hustler said, "With no wings, I fly. With no eyes, I see. With no arms, I climb. More frightening than any beast, stronger than any foe. I am cunning, ruthless, and tall. In the end, I rule all."

I stared. I had no idea. *I fly, I see, I climb.* How'd I get myself into this mess? *Cunning, ruthless, and tall?*

"C'mon, lass," someone said.

"I…" I shook my head. *In the end, I rule all?* "I don't

know."

"Give the lady a minute, now," said the round-faced man with the kind smile.

My mind was blank. "Really," I said, "I have no idea. I'm sorry."

Outsmarted by Mr. Potato Head. Could my day get any worse?

The hustler grinned wide and swept the cash off the bar and into his pocket. "Sorry, men."

"Now wait just a minute," said the bearded man, rising from his stool. His blue eyes flared with rage. "Why do I feel like we just been swindled by you two?"

"What? No." I shook my head.

His fury wasn't focused on the hustler, but me. The other three men fell in behind him.

"I didn't have anything to—"

The hustler started to slip from his stool.

I nudged him in the shoulder with my finger. "Where do you think you're going?"

The four men turned to him. His buggy eyes darted from one to the other as he assessed his foes.

I said to him, "I'm pretty sure what you just pulled isn't legal. So go on, give these men their money back and call it a day."

He smirked and stood taller. "I'll do no such thing." He looked to the barkeep as he adjusted his collar and smoothed his shirt sleeves. "It was a fair bet."

"Maybe we should let the police sort it out," I suggested to the bearded man.

The hustler grabbed me by the arm and shoved me against the bar. He probably stood about five-ten, two-hundred pounds of net-hauling muscle. "Maybe you should mind your own business, sweetheart."

This guy was really starting to piss me off. I looked down at his hand, then looked him in the eye, and, with a smile pasted on my face, my voice all dripping with syrup, said, "Take your hand off me or I'll break it."

This seemed to encourage him more. "That's not very ladylike," he grunted through gritted teeth.

I matched his stare. "I'm not sure you know how to treat a lady."

"What's this? Part of your act?" the bearded man bellowed.

The hustler glanced at the door, the quickest of glances, but I caught it. He was going to bolt.

He shoved me into the bar and I reacted. I jabbed my elbow upward at his throat, extended my arm, gave his head a twist, and knocked him off his feet. He stumbled to catch his balance, but I had my foot on top of his. He teetered forward and, with a little help from my hand, face-planted into the edge of the bar. *Take that.* I brushed off my hands and wiped my brow. *Mashed potato.*

From his pocket, I pulled out the wad of cash and handed it to the bearded man. He responded with a bewildered expression, staring open-mouthed at the money as though it had magically shimmered into existence right there in his hand.

The hustler crumpled to the floor.

I picked up my Beamish. "Thanks for the grog," I said and held it up in salute.

The four men exchanged glances, unsure whether this was still part of some elaborate con.

The barkeep tapped me on the shoulder. "Out."

"What? Me?" I glanced down at the hustler, now sitting upright on the floor holding his head. "He's the one who—"

The gruff old barkeep jabbed his finger at me. "I'm not going to ask you twice."

Dammit. I didn't even get to enjoy the beer.

I slinked out the front door.

As I walked down the wooden-plank sidewalk, I spotted Dalton coming my way.

"What's going on?" he asked, his face wrinkled with

concern.

"Nothing. I just—" I clenched my teeth together. "I just got kicked out of the pub is all."

A grin spread across his face and his eyes lit with amusement. "Seriously?"

I wanted to punch him in the stomach. "Enjoy the moment."

"What on earth happened—wait, I probably don't want to know." His eyes closed shut, then the grin took over again. He blinked them open. "Anything I should know?"

"No," I said with a frown.

He shook his head and snickered. "I'll meet you back at the lodge."

I watched him saunter away, grinning all the way to the pub, the pub where I was supposed to be hunkered down in a dark corner to keep watch.

I headed down the wharf to walk it off. A couple of tall ships were docked, their wooden masts bedangled with complicated rigging. I'd always wanted to sail aboard one of those old ships, flying the Jolly Roger and spitting into the wind. Maybe drink rum from a wooden cask. I couldn't go for the eye patch, but a pet parrot would be fun. I could teach him to swear with an Irish accent.

I sat down on the edge of the pier and let my legs dangle over the water. A couple of gulls skittered into the air, then circled back to perch on the pilings and the stench of backwater and diesel fumes wafted my way.

Of course I wouldn't have a pet parrot. And some kind of partner I was. Dalton was in there alone right now, with no backup. Sure, the risk was low, but still. It was my job. And he was my partner. All because I'd misjudged the scene. And then I opened my big mouth. I wouldn't blame Dalton if he sent me home tonight.

I grinned in spite of myself. That ass deserved to get clobbered. And by a girl, as he would say. That probably really pissed him off. Thought he was so clever with his riddles. *Cunning, ruthless, and tall.*

"Imagination!" I shouted to the gulls. *Dammit.* Head slap. *Now it comes to me.*

About four hours after Dalton went in, the warm light spilled out into the dark alley as he came out the front door of the pub and headed toward our lodge. I stepped from the shadows and followed him. Made it two blocks before he spotted me.

"I thought I said I'd meet you back at the pension," he said.

I shrugged him off. "I wanted to hang close. In case you needed me."

"Uh, huh," he said. "So how'd you get yourself banished anyway?"

"Some old man had grabby paws." It was only a half fib.

Dalton grinned. "You're something, you know that?"

"Whatever." I gave him the look. "Did our informant show?"

He shook his head. "Waited all this time. Then the bartender hands me this note."

He held it out for me to read. *Fish Market, 10 a.m. Two days. Come alone.*

"*Two days.* But Ray Goldman is out there, somewhere, right now. We need to get going. We need to know which direction."

Dalton sauntered along, unaffected.

I kicked a tiny chunk of concrete that had crumbled from the edge of the curb and watched it skitter down the sidewalk. "We don't have two days to wait."

Dalton stopped and turned to face me. "Patience, my dear."

"Don't patronize me. You know time's a factor here. We've got a tiny window to catch this guy. If he gets a whale before we catch up to him, he'll sail off into the sunset, to sell it in Russia or China or Timbuktu. He'll be beyond our reach. Don't you care?"

His hands went to his hips. "Of course I care."

"Well, how can you be so—"

"You're so cute when you're angry."

My bottom lip was sticking out. I sucked it back in. "Cute!" A rush of color heated my cheeks. *Errrrr!*

"I want to catch this guy as badly as you do," he said, calm as can be. "But some things are out of our control."

"So, what? You're saying we wait around and do nothing?"

"You don't like cold coffee and stale doughnuts?"

"Dalton!"

"Actually, I have an idea." He grinned. "I think you'll like it."

I didn't like the sound of this.

"When I was a SEAL, we used down time for training, trust building, that kind of thing. We could use a little of that."

"Like a little of what?"

A grin spread across his face. The hint of challenge in his eyes made me nervous.

CHAPTER 2

I leaned out over the granite ledge and gazed down at the fjord 3,208 feet below. A white sheen of glistening sunlight spread across the greenish-blue water. Two endangered Eurasian peregrine falcons swooped and soared on the wind below us. One caught a thermal and gently glided into a circular flight path, its wings outstretched. The fastest animal on Earth, a falcon can dive over 200 miles per hour. I don't know how Dalton knew, but I'd been wanting to see one for as long as I could remember.

At last, there were two in my sights. But today we weren't here just to see them. We were going to soar with them. If they'd have us.

"You ready?" I asked Dalton.

He nodded and smiled, the dimple in his right cheek appearing. "You're the one who's been lollygagging."

"I want to time it just right." I shaded my eyes with my hand and searched for the sliver of grassy shoreline onto which I was supposed to land. "See you on terra firma."

I ran back to where my paraglider wing lay in the grass, clipped it to my harness, then gave it a yank. It lifted from the ground, filling with air. I turned and ran and as I reached the edge, I was airborne, held aloft by the warm ridge-lift air current.

My breath left my body as the great expanse of the fjord

spread below me, the cliffs on either side narrowing downward. No matter how many times I did this, it still took my breath away.

As I glided outward, I felt a slight uplift and shifted to catch the thermal, which lifted me up and up as I circled.

I scanned below for the falcons. There was the one I'd seen, its wings spread wide, still riding on a thermal below. I leaned right, yanked on my brake, and went into a sharp, spiraling, tickle-belly descent, heading toward the bird on a corkscrew path. I dropped about a hundred meters in eight seconds.

I released the inner brake, shifted left, and planed out.

Curious, the falcon flapped its wings and cut right, circling to get a look at me. I spread my arms wide. "Come fly with me!"

I entered the core of the thermal and caught some serious lift. As I circled, Dalton appeared, riding on the wind beside me.

The two falcons darted between us, banked and soared upward, then circled back and streaked past like feathered bullets.

I grabbed my radio. "Oh my god! That was incredible!"

Dalton gave me a thumbs up.

Now I could relax and enjoy the view. Blue sky dotted with tiny, white puffy clouds contrasted with the jagged granite peaks. Below, strokes of green, white, brown and yellow covered the landscape—an abstract painting come alive. I settled into the peacefulness of no sound save for the breeze against my ears. It was perfection.

Between my feet, a tiny spec of a boat left a wake on the water's surface, a white line etched in blue. Amid the patches of green that spread across the mountain side, little dots of white randomly roamed. Billy goats.

I leaned back and breathed deeply the cool, clean air. To ride on the wind, to soar like a bird, to see the world from this perspective, in pure solitude, where I was the spec, the tiny dot, made me wonder, is this what it is to know God? Or the spiritual essence some call God, that something beyond, the unexplainable sensation of being more than flesh and bone?

Is this what was meant by transcendence? To defy the law of gravity? To be held aloft by an invisible force of nature like some great hand, lifted from below? What is the wind but an illusion, made manifest by the collision of hot and cold air?

However it could be explained, it felt like touching the divine.

I closed my eyes and when I opened them again the colors looked deeper, more vivid. So many varied shades of green. The blue of the water, rich and deep against the sky. Simplicity. The purest form of beauty.

Dalton's voice came over the radio. "Last one to the LZ buys dinner."

He pushed on his speed bar, leaned left, and shot away, circling downward toward the landing zone.

I grabbed my B-lines and went into a stall, chasing after him. Like two giant raptors, we rode the wind downward.

He dropped away from me, gaining speed. The wind was perfect, the sun shining. Why rush?

Okay, fine. I admit. It grinded my butt that he got the drop on me. There was no way I could catch him now. Another dinner on me. Maybe he'd go for some peanut butter and jelly.

I controlled my descent, taking my time to plan my approach. As I lined up into the wind, Dalton was already touching down.

The landing site was a grassy patch along the shoreline. I circled to head into the wind and as I approached the ground, I pulled a quick brake, flared, then my feet touched the ground and I had to run a few steps to stay upright as the wing settled behind me.

"Took you long enough," Dalton hollered.

He was wrapping his wing and stuffing it into the sack.

I had a mind to stuff his head in the sack. "We have enough

daylight to make one more run," I said. "Double or nothing?"

He shook his head. "We need to check in with Nash."

I nodded. Work. Of course. That's why we were here in Norway. But we had nothing new to report. We'd have called if Johnny the informant had changed the meet time again.

Dalton flipped on the flashing light that would alert the ferry of a pickup, then helped me gather my wing.

We hauled our packs to the shoreline and sat down to wait. My pulse was finally settling to normal after the glide. I'd stripped off my thick coat after landing, but now the chilly breeze coming off the water gave me goosebumps on my bare arms.

Dalton sat with his arms comfortably wrapped around his knees. His hair looked almost blond in the sun. A hint of stubble showed on his chin. Suddenly I was remembering watching him shave in Costa Rica, fresh from the shower, with nothing on but a towel. He hadn't liked me much then. I'd been sent to fortify his cover story in a floundering operation and he wasn't too happy about it. I'd barreled into the bathroom and demanded he talk to me.

"What are you thinking about?"

"What?" I snapped out of my reverie.

"You seemed a million miles away."

"Oh, sorry, I…" I looked up at the sky, searching for a subject. "When you're up there, do you, I don't know, do you feel like—" I looked around "— like with all this, there's something greater, you know—"

He raised an eyebrow, his dark eyes challenging me. "Are you getting soft on me, McVie?"

"Nah," I snorted. "I was just testing you."

He shook his head but his eyes lingered in the clouds. Then when they met mine, they revealed that he felt it too.

I held his gaze for a moment. *This guy, I swear.* I turned away.

"Here it comes now," he said. The ferry was chugging down

the fjord toward us.

We got to our feet and hauled our packs onto our backs.

The blue and white ferry pulled up and dropped its front loading ramp right on shore so we could walk on.

Once aboard, Dalton slumped to the floor, leaned on his pack, and closed his eyes. I stayed at the rail, counting waterfalls as we puttered back toward town. The landscape here was too much to behold. I turned to Dalton, "You're missing the—"

His eyes were open; he was staring at me.

"What?" I said.

He smiled. "Nothing."

"Don't you want to see the scenery?"

"I'm full. Too much beauty for one day."

I suddenly felt self-conscious of how I must've looked and ran my fingers through my tangled hair. "What are you talking about, cornball?"

"Nothing."

"Hey, what was this exercise all about? What was I supposed to learn today, anyway?"

"Did you have fun?"

I shrugged, unsure what that had to do with it. "Yeah."

"There you go." He closed his eyes again. "Now, leave me be. I'm dreaming of that dinner you owe me. I'm gonna order a big, juicy steak."

I milled around the fish market, keeping Dalton in view while checking out every man that looked like he might be our Johnny. Then the guy appeared out of nowhere, wearing a hoodie, his back to me. Dalton didn't look uncomfortable or alarmed, so I hung back, scanning for anything out of the ordinary.

The whole conversation lasted no more than two minutes and he was gone. I never saw his face.

Dalton moved toward me. "The description fits. It's Ray

Goldman all right. He's been busy getting a crew together and all the gear he'll need. No doubt about it. This guy's sure he's going after orcas."

My pulse pitter-pattered in my ears. "We gotta catch him, Dalton. This one's big. Imagine the impact it will have, the message it will send to all the poachers out there."

"Simmer down. We've got to find him first. The informant said he's in Tromsø right now, on the fishing vessel *Forseti*, but he's not sure which way he'll set sail. We need to get up there, find him, and rent a boat before we lose his trail."

"What then? We just follow him? That's your plan? Won't we be too obvious?"

"What else did you think we'd do?"

"Well." I pursed my lips, thinking. "I don't suppose Norway requires AIS on all commercial vessels? We could track him that way but keep our distance."

"I doubt it. That would be too easy. Besides, he'd likely turn it off anyway. It's a big ocean. Easy to hide if you don't want to be found."

"If only we could get away with planting a GPS tracker on his boat."

He stopped and turned to face me. "We'd have to be awfully creative and I'm not sure—"

My head jerked back. "Isn't that illegal? No matter how we did it?"

He gave me a half shrug.

An idea sizzled through my gray matter. "Maybe we don't have to. Follow the boat, I mean." *Why didn't I think of this before?*

Dalton clenched his teeth. "I recognize that look."

"What?"

"You're thinking. Scheming." He crossed his arms. "Let's get something straight. We're going to work together on this one. Do you understand? No secrets, no sneaking around."

"I wasn't—"

"And nothing off book. You got it?"

I lifted my hands in innocent surrender. I couldn't blame him for being irritated with me. In Costa Rica, our first time working together, I hadn't exactly been straight with him. Of course, he hadn't quite rolled out the red carpet for me either. But now we were officially partners. He had to listen to me.

"I was just thinking that the orca pods don't follow a predictable migration route like other whales."

Dalton waited, expectantly. "Yeah, so?"

"Well, I wonder how Ray plans to find them. Did your pal Johnny mention that?"

Dalton shook his head.

"I've got an idea," I said. "We need the Internet." I turned to make my way out of the crowded fish market and head toward the main street.

Dalton grabbed my arm. "First, you tell me what you're thinking."

"Maybe we don't need to follow Ray," I said and started walking again.

Dalton followed. "Slow down," he said. "It's not a race."

"Actually, it is," I said over my shoulder. I rounded a corner and saw a sign—Internettkafè—down one block. I picked up the pace, Dalton on my heels.

Inside the cafè, teenagers filled the booths and tables, plunking away at their laptops, sipping from cups of coffee as the expresso machine squealed, making its magical brew. The scent of fresh muffins lingered.

I went straight for an open computer along the wall and plopped down in the chair. Dalton hovered over my shoulder, so close I could smell his aftershave. For a moment, I forgot what I wanted to search. "Maybe you could get us some coffee," I said.

He stood up straight and glared at me.

I gave him a sweet smile. "And some of those mørkaker shortbread cookies?" My eyebrows went up, a gentle pleading.

"They are to die for."

He crossed his arms. "Not until you fill me in."

"It's like I said, if we find the orcas, we find Ray."

"Yeah?" He didn't budge.

"I figure *someone* knows where to find them. Must be scientists monitoring the pods, right? Identifying their members, documenting their behavior."

The corner of his mouth turned up with the hint of a smile. "Mørkaker shortbread cookies, huh?"

I nodded.

He slowly turned away from me and headed for the line.

When he got back, I'd already found what I was looking for. "Look," I said. "Right here."

I pointed to the page for the Center for Marine Research at the Havforskningsinstituttet.

"Now there's a Norwegian word if I've ever seen one. It's ten miles long," he said.

"I think you mean ten kilometers." I looked up at him. "They're hosting an American biologist, here to study the vocalizations of killer whales. April Parker, Ph.D. If anyone knows right where to find killer whales in the north Atlantic, it'll be her."

"Yeah, but will she tell us?"

Chapter 3

The cafeteria at the Havforskningsinstituttet bustled with students. Dalton and I meandered through the crowd looking for Dr. Parker. Her Internet picture was no help. She was all bundled up in a down jacket with a hood and sunglasses. We'd checked in her department where we were told she was at lunch.

"When we find her, I think I should approach her alone," I said. "She's likely to be more trusting of another woman."

"Actually," Dalton said. "I was thinking I'd approach her alone. I have more experience with this kind of thing."

"That might be," I said, holding back, "but the key is to build trust right away, right? I can do that, you know, woman to woman."

"This is going to take some finesse."

"Finesse?" I said, amused.

"Charm," he said.

I pressed my lips tight, trying to squelch a smile. "Dalton, I think you overestimate your—"

"We only have one shot at this," he said, his voice stern now. "I'm doing it."

I spun on him. "Dalton, you're not being reasonable. Just admit I'm right."

He got that look on his face. Man, this guy could be stubborn. Through a forced smile he said, "It's not about being right."

Then the condescending grin. "It's about the line of command. Or have you forgotten who's the senior agent?"

"So it's not about what's most effective? It's about who's in charge?"

He sighed. Thought about it a moment. "Yes."

"Fine," I said, holding back an eye roll. "Now, let's find her."

He nodded toward a table in the corner. "She's right over there."

Sitting with her head down, a fork in one hand, a book open in the other, was a woman not much older than me, her long blond hair tied back into a stylish Chinese bun, two hair sticks poking out from it, criss-crossed.

I spun on him. "How do you—"

He held his phone in my face. "Her DMV photo. Nash sent it."

"What? You knew she was there all along?" I frowned. "What is it with you today?"

He flashed his half-grin.

I asked, "So what are you going to say?"

"I've got it covered."

"She could be informing for Goldman, you know. I'm sure he'd pay big money for that kind of info. Maybe we should test the waters a little and—"

"I said, I've got it covered." He brushed past me and crossed the room to her table.

I circled around, eased into a chair at a table nearby so I could hear their conversation, and tried not to stare. Flawless skin, high cheekbones, curvy, voluptuous lips. I hadn't expected a whale biologist to be so…so stunning.

"Hello," he said. "Are you Dr. Parker, the whale researcher?"

She looked up at him, hesitating. "Yes," she finally said as she tucked a stray lock of blond hair behind her ear.

He flashed his tummy-tingling smile. "I was hoping you

might be able to help me."

Her brow creased and she examined him through squinted eyes. She had the look of a porcelain doll, but this woman was no naive little plaything.

He shifted his weight to one side, easing into a comfortable, disarming stance. "You're even prettier in person."

Real smooth, Dalton.

"What is it you need?" she said, blank-faced.

He smiled, trying to keep it light. "I hear you're the expert on the killer whale population here in Norway and I—"

She shook her head. "I can't help you."

"Oh," he said. "I was really hoping you—"

"Listen—" she gripped her lunch tray "—I don't know what you're up to, but no amount of money—"

"Oh no, ma'am, I think you misunderstand," he said, then shot a quick glance my way. "I'm a federal agent with the U.S. Fish and Wildlife service." He motioned for me to join him. "We've been alerted to a possible live capture attempt by an American here in Norwegian waters."

Her sharp blue eyes darted back and forth between us, then landed on me. "You don't look like federal agents. Show me your badges."

Dalton shifted on his feet. "We don't carry badges when we're undercover."

"Well, that's convenient." She grabbed her tray and started to rise to go.

Dalton stepped forward with open hands, a subtle gesture of peace. "We'll do whatever you ask to prove it to you."

She hesitated, her eyes back on me.

"Please." He held his hand out in an invitation to sit back down.

She set the tray down, but remained standing. To me she said, "You said *U.S.* Fish and Wildlife. Why would you be here, in Norway?"

"We're after a notorious criminal, top of our most wanted

list."

She stared, unsatisfied. This woman was not short on intelligence.

I went on. "The Marine Mammal Protection Act of 1972 prohibits hunting, capturing, killing or even harassing any marine mammal in U.S. Waters *or*—" I paused for effect "—or by U.S. citizens *anywhere* in the world."

"You're clever," she said crossing her arms. "But not clever enough."

I smiled. Held up my hands. Of course she would know this would normally be handled by NOAA agents. "You mean, of course, because the MMPA is the purview of NOAA. We're here as part of a joint effort with their enforcement agency. They're concerned that the suspect would recognize most of their agents, so here we are. This is a high profile case, you know, with the news lately—" I smiled at her "—and politics. Orcas are very popular and a protected species so—"

"Of course I know that." She let her hands fall to the table and, with one finger, slowly spun her plate a quarter turn. "This is my life's work."

I let out my breath. She was warming to us. "We need to find this guy before he finds the whales so we can catch him in the act. If we miss that tiny window of opportunity, he'll get away with it. Please help us stop him."

Dalton added, "We don't know who else to turn to for help."

She looked into Dalton's eyes and held his gaze for what seemed a bit longer than necessary before she said, "You don't have the eyes of a killer." She sank into the chair and pushed the tray out of her way. "I've been afraid of this."

"How do you mean?" Dalton asked as he eased into the chair across from her.

"You've been approached, haven't you?" I said.

She didn't respond, but I could tell I was right. "Oceanaria. It's a dirty word if you ask me. We should be destroying these—" she shuddered "—these prisons, not building more. Do you know what happens to them in captivity?" She didn't wait for a response. "They're crammed into chlorinated tanks with bare concrete walls, forced to perform circus tricks under neon lights with horrible music blasting over the loud speakers. No wonder they show signs of aggression. To claim that having killer whales in captivity is teaching us anything about them and their natural behavior is absurd. If anything, all we're learning is what happens when you enslave a sentient being."

I smiled and nodded, hoping to convey my sincerity. Listening to her describe the horrors of captivity stirred my anger and made me feel more desperate to gain her trust.

"We'd been hearing rumors of new demand for wild captures. I had hoped it was just that, rumors, until…" She looked down at her half-eaten sandwich and frowned. "The breeding loan program is a farce. That's the problem. Breeding in captivity has been mostly unsuccessful. They breed them too young, and they're matching whales that are too genetically-close, all causing an unnatural percentage of stillborn calves. With demand for more orcas in marine parks around the world—Russia, China, and Japan—they have to fill those tanks from somewhere."

"Exactly," I said. "And with Norway's political—"

"That's if the whales actually survive being captured. It's awful you know. Many die from the trauma. Not just physical, but emotional." Her lip quivered, ever so slightly. I got the sense she was holding back tears. I felt for her. A scientist would be criticized for being too emotional about her subjects. "Orcas have strong family bonds. When one is captured, it's agonizing for the entire pod. But imagine for the one captured, being lifted from the water, what that must feel like, while your family members are wailing in distress." She covered her mouth with her hand. "It's inhumane."

Dalton gave her his warmest smile. "We're going to do

everything we can."

She went on, her focus on Dalton. "If only they'd been called the pandas of the sea. The name, killer whale, comes from a time of ignorance and fear. They're not mindless, brutal killers, you know. They're highly intelligent beings. Clever and amazingly adaptive. What we've learned about them from their vocalizations alone is—"

She went silent and pursed her lips. I don't know how she didn't burst into tears. I was on the verge of blubbering myself.

Dalton and I exchanged a quick glance.

She sighed and forced a smile. "You said you received a tip on a live capture attempt?"

"Yes," Dalton said. "But we're not clear on how accurate it is or up-to-date. The informant said our man's sailing near Tromsø."

"Tromsø?" She took hold of the lunch tray, a determination in her posture. "We should go to my lab."

Sunshine streamed through a two-story wall of glass, bathing the Cetacean Research lab in warmth. No back-corner basement rooms dimly lit with sickly-green fluorescents here. The architecture was all glass and sleek lines—distinctly Scandinavian.

A long counter ran along the opposite wall, its surface cluttered with bones of assorted cetaceans, stacks of plastic trays, and boxes of tools. On one end of the room, several desks housed computers and on the wall, photos of whales, all grouped by pods, it seemed, were pinned to a giant map of Norway.

Dr. Parker strode to the wall, her willowy frame carrying her like a model down a Paris runway. She swept her hand across the map. "There are about 3,000 killer whales in Norwegian waters. Half live in the Barents Sea and up around Svalbard.

That covers a great area of open sea, very remote, so I doubt your—" she hesitated as though trying to find the right word "—*criminal* would target that area. Along the coast and out in the Norwegian Sea, however, offer him a lot of opportunity. Tromsø isn't the best staging port. Too far from the migration paths. If he's there now, he's probably getting crew and supplies and planning to move on."

Move on to where, I wanted to ask, but she seemed on a roll, so I didn't want to interrupt the flow of words.

"All killer whale migration, across every ocean in the world, is tied to their prey, which varies from pod to pod. A pod is a complex and cohesive family group. Here in the North Atlantic, there are two distinct types of killer whale pods, transients and residents. Resident pods tend to have a defined home range, which would make them most vulnerable. Transients travel over considerable distances hunting marine mammals, making them a little harder to find."

Dalton, hanging on her every word, asked, "So you can easily locate the resident pods? They follow a certain pattern?"

She paused as though seeing him for the first time. Her eyes traveled up and down his body. A flirty smile skipped across her lips. "Not exactly. The main prey of killer whales in Norwegian waters is spring-spawning herring. The herring don't follow any certain pattern."

I thought so. "But are they—"

"So find the herring, find the killer whales," Dalton interrupted, his eyes glued to her.

"Yes, you're right, very good," she said, smiling at Dalton like he was her star student, then turned her attention to the map once again. "The herring used to migrate every fall like clockwork into Vestfjord near Lofoten,"—she ran her hand along the map, her finger landing on, then tapping at the Lofoten islands—"but in recent years the herring stock changed its migration pattern and has been wintering in the open ocean, north and northwest of the Lofoten islands." Her hand swirled, motioning out to sea. "It's made our research more difficult, that's for sure. The whales, when we do see them, are traveling fast and in an unpredictable fashion. In the last three years, we've only spotted them in Andfjord."

Dalton stepped closer to her. "So you're saying their feeding habits have changed?"

"No, just the locations. Their feeding technique, which is a specialized technique seen only in these waters, is called carousel feeding. Their ingenuity is quite impressive, actually. In close cooperation with each other, the whales will chase the herring school into a tight ball formation close to the water's surface. They then slap the herring ball with their tails, stunning them, making it easy to pick off the fish one by one.

"A carousel feeding event can be exciting to watch and seems quite chaotic. The herring jump out of the water, huge numbers of birds descend on them, and the whales often make high, arched dives. Below water, though, it's apparent, it's a carefully choreographed maneuver. And the vocalizations during the event—" She paused, shaking her head in awe.

Her fascination with these creatures was contagious. I wanted to see this feeding event, to witness the excitement, to hear them communicating.

Her gaze became unfocused as though she'd fixed on some distant thought.

"That's amazing," Dalton said, bringing her back.

"Wait a minute," she said to no one, her eyes scanning the board. She rushed to a computer, plunked at the keys, her eyes darting about the monitor. "Oh no." She looked up from the screen. "I think I know which pod he's going after."

Dalton and I glanced at each other. My heart rate picked up. "Which one? Why?"

"The K-pod." She covered her eyes with her hands. "Dammit! I should have realized."

"What?" Dalton asked. "You should have realized what?"

"Last week. My assistant went on a date. It went badly.

She said the guy wouldn't shut up about the whales. It took her awhile to realize, that's all the creep wanted. When she told me about it"—she flung her head back and stared up at the ceiling—"I figured he was an environmental reporter or something."

Dalton said, "We need to talk to this assistant."

Dr. Parker nodded. "That's fine but, that's what made me realize. Trust me, they're going after the K-pod." She launched from the chair, back to the board, pointing at a photo. "K-12 has a nursing calf. That slows the whole pod down, making them an easier target. Plus this pod has several adolescents, the primary target for wild-caught captives. They're strong and healthy…exactly what…" She plopped back into the chair. Her shoulders sagged as though grief was already setting in. "He'll be able to easily herd them." She shook her head. "He'll have his pick."

"Not if we get to him first," Dalton said.

"The K-pod is…" Her eyes locked with Dalton's. "Very special."

"Why?" I asked, fighting to keep my own emotions in check.

"All killer whales form matrilineal groups, that is, all are offspring of one female. Even the male killer whales stay in their birth family for their entire life. Except to go mate, of course."

Did she just raise an eyebrow at Dalton?

"We know of no other creature where all children—daughters and sons—stay with their mother all her life." She looked at me as if she'd noticed me for the first time since we entered her lab. "Can you imagine that kind of family bond?"

I shook my head. I couldn't imagine wanting to stay with my mom. My dad maybe, but my mom, no way.

"Anyway," she went on, her attention back on Dalton, her smile returning. "A large pod might be made up of a couple of these groups. In the K-pod, K-4, we call her Granny K, is eighty years old. She saw too many of her loved ones ripped from her family back in the 1970s and 80s when this particular pod was targeted for capture. Over half of the family was taken. They've been struggling to regain a sustainable number ever since. The new calf, well,—" a pink blush came to her cheeks and she gave Dalton a conspiratorial wink "—I call her Baby Kimmy, she's the first we've seen in several years." She drew in a sharp breath. Her eyes lit with fear. "If he takes Kimmy's mom—"

"All right," Dalton said in a soothing voice. "Let's not get ahead of ourselves."

She shot up from the chair. "You can't let this happen. You can't."

"Okay, okay." He was nodding.

She eyed Dalton with the ferocious glare of a mother bear. "What are you going to do about it?"

"Well," he said. "First we have to locate the suspect. Then we'll take video of the capture. Once we have the evidence in hand, we'll call the Norwegian authorities. They'll make an arrest and we'll have him extradited to the U.S. for prosecution."

"Why don't you call the Norwegian authorities now?"

"Well," he gave her a placating smile. "We need to first confirm it is indeed Ray Goldman and that he is here with the intent to capture a killer whale. Whaling politics here in Norway have been—"

"Yeah, I know," she said. "But what he's doing is illegal here. Why do you need video? That means you have to actually stand by and let him capture one, right? Can't you just arrest him when it's clear that's what he's going to do?"

"We don't have the authority to arrest him here. Since we're not sure which way the Norwegian government would sway, we want our own evidence to convict him. The distinction is important."

"Not to the whale it's not."

I had the same thought. "Exactly," I said. I didn't want to lose her now that we were finally getting somewhere. "The whales are our first priority. That's why the timing is so important."

Her eyes flicked back and forth, from him to me.

"We'll get this guy," Dalton said. He paused, waited, looking at her with those eyes. "That is, with your help."

We waited while she chewed on her lip, her eyes fixed on some distant space.

"So," I said, easing back into the discussion. "The whales are likely to be in Andfjord then? That's where we should look?"

"Huh?" She looked up at me, her eyes shifting into focus. "What?"

"Andfjord? You said that's where they'd likely be?"

She shook her head and plopped back down in the chair. "Oh no. They're not there."

What the hell? "I thought you just said—"

Her fingers hammered at the keyboard. "If your whale hunter is in Tromsø, he's got miles to go. My guess, if he knows what he's doing, he'll arrive in the Lofoten Islands within a few days. You should go to Reine. The K-pod has been south of there and they're turning back north."

"How can you be sure?"

She said, matter-of-fact, "Granny K is satellite-tagged."

CHAPTER 4

We hopped on a train north, then a quick flight, then the ferry to the tiny, historic fishing village of Reine. Right out of a Scandinavian fairy tale, granite peaks jut straight up out of the blue-green sea. Bright red fishermen's cabins with grass roofs dot the rocky shoreline, suspended in time on their wooden stilts, the sea splashing below the floorboards. In the middle of it all, Stetind peak dominates the skyline. Norwegians call it *gudenes ambolt*, the "anvil of the gods," because its summit looks as though it had been lopped clean off, leaving a flat, level precipice.

First thing, we walked the docks, but saw no sign of the *Forseti*. I asked Dalton. "So how do you want to play this?"

"We rent a boat, a newly married couple on holiday"—he winked at me—"and make sure all the video equipment is charged and rigged. When we get a fix on him, we'll keep him in our sights as much as possible and stay in direct communication with April."

"April? You mean, Dr. Parker."

"Yeah, that's what I meant."

"I thought your approach was real smooth by the way. *You're even prettier in person*," I said with a wink. "I don't know what her problem was. You'd have had me at hello."

Dalton crossed his arms. "So you're going to gloat?"

"Just for a while," I said with a victorious grin. We turned toward town. "Do you really think Goldman will be so bold as to try to take a whale with another boat close enough to witness it?"

He shrugged. "If not, we've come a long way for nothing."

I frowned. There had to be a better way. Right now, I couldn't think of one. Not one that stayed within the law anyway.

I shot off a text to Dr. Parker to let her know we'd arrived and there was no sign of Ray Goldman yet, hoping she'd keep her word and send us regular updates on the K-pod's movements.

Without knowing exactly what to expect, we weren't sure what would be the best vessel for our needs. Finally, we decided on a cruising sailboat, figuring worst-case-scenario, running out of gas wouldn't be life-threatening.

We managed to find a company that rented pleasure craft to tourists. Conveniently, nearly everyone in Norway speaks English, even in this tiny village, and we were able to get exactly what we wanted.

The *Sea Mist* she was called. A forty-foot sloop with two cabins, one head, and a nice galley with a deep-freeze. The salon was paneled in teak and smelled of the sea, as a boat should. The seat cushions had been updated with an aquamarine and imperial blue striped fabric. Every door and drawer bore a white sticker listing the contents and an *In Case of Emergency* poster had been stapled on the wall above the main radio controls.

The owner, a friendly local with an easy-going demeanor, gave us an hour-long orientation that included personal tales of his adventures on a sailboat. When his stories ran out, he wanted to see our ASA certification or some kind of documentation to be sure we were qualified to sail a vessel this size. Being a Navy SEAL, Dalton would be given the helm no problem, I'm sure, but this was a small community and we had to be careful what we revealed. To them, we were a married couple on holiday.

"Gee, I didn't think to bring anything," Dalton said,

stalling.

"Perhaps you could quiz us, to satisfy your requirements?" I suggested.

The man shrugged. "Um, okay. How much rode do you put out to anchor safely? I believe that is the English word, rode."

"Yes, you are correct," I said. "Rope or chain?"

"Rope."

"Seven to one scope."

I could feel Dalton's eyes on me.

"All right," the man said. "If two sailboats on the same tack are approaching one another, which is the give-way vessel?"

"The windward vessel," I said. "It should alter course to pass astern of the stand-on vessel."

He stared at me for a moment, then turned to Dalton. "It's late in the season to be out on the water."

"We came to see the whales," I said.

"You're going to pay the balance up front?"

We nodded.

"Have a good time," he said with a dismissive wave and went back into his shed.

Off to the grocery store we headed to fill our stocks. We had no idea how long we'd be on board, what amount of supplies we'd need, so I loaded the cart to the brim with canned vegetables and boxes of crackers while Dalton wandered around the store picking up packages of mystery foods.

"What was that back there? You've been on a sailboat?" Dalton asked as we crossed in front of the frozen food section.

Does he think I was born yesterday? "Nah, I learned all that from an episode of the Brady Bunch. Greg and Marsha wanted to sail to India and—"

He crinkled up his brow.

Fine. "I spent a summer on one once. With my dad." It was the best summer of my life. Just me and my dad and the sea. No one telling us what to do, how to live. If I could go back to one time in my life… "I was twelve. Four months we sailed the Pacific coast, from Vancouver to Alaska. My dad had made some deal with a Navy buddy and voilà, we were living on a boat."

"You remembered the anchor scope and right-of-way rules from when you were twelve?"

I shrugged. "That summer is etched in my memory."

He waited.

I looked up at him. "It was my last summer with my dad."

He nodded in understanding. "Before he was killed."

I nodded. "The irony is, when he was planning it, my mother never shut up about it, going on and on about how dangerous it would be." I paused. If only we'd stayed on that boat. He never would have—I couldn't go there. Not right now with Dalton. I laughed, keeping it light. "I admit, I wasn't sure it would float at first, but once my dad and I were on the water, it was like I'd gone home. The serenity of the sea, the simplicity of a single-minded focus, going where the wind took us. I learned so much that summer."

"I bet," he said.

"I didn't exactly have a typical childhood."

"No kidding?" He shrugged. "They're overrated anyway."

I grinned. "I sailed the high seas, swimming with dolphins and singing in the wind."

"Explains a lot."

I elbowed him in the gut. "What about you?" I asked. "You know how to handle a sailboat?"

He raised one eyebrow.

"Oh right, you were a SEAL. You've done everything."

"Not everything," he said with a sly grin. "On a sailboat, that is."

He held my gaze until I turned away with a huff. "Oh, you are incorrigible."

The next morning, still no sign of the *Forseti*. We were lounging in the cockpit with cups of coffee and, though I'd done my morning yoga, I was feeling restless. The surrounding peaks beckoned. I must have been gazing up at them, my ankles twitching, because Dalton asked, "You up for a hike?"

"We can't leave the marina. What if—"

"If the *Forseti* arrives, he's going to stay at least one night to resupply."

"I don't think we should risk missing him."

"You're probably right," he said. "Unless..." He gestured toward the mountain peaks. "I bet, from up there, we could see any boat coming or going for miles."

I grinned. "I like the way you think." I pointed to the highest peak. "How about we try that one?"

"Is there even a trail, do you think?" he asked.

"Why? Do you need one?"

With a curt shake of his head, he said, "Just to keep track of you, McVie." He tossed the magazine he'd been reading aside and rose from the seat. "Let's go."

He offered to pack our lunch while I walked the docks one more time to be sure we hadn't missed the arrival of the *Forseti* while we'd slept. Within fifteen minutes, we were on our way.

There was indeed a trail, we found out. At the end of a short road, an arrow had been painted on the concrete, pointing to the trailhead.

We ducked into the foliage, single-file, and started an easy ascent.

The air was crisp, the piney scent of the forest refreshing. The morning sun warmed my back. For the first five hundred yards or more we walked on a solid plate of rock, then the hillside sloped upward and the trail turned to a rich, dark soil cut through thick grasses and low bushes. The path switched back and forth through a forest of alders and birches, the ground covered in a blanket of ferns and dotted with the occasional purple of bluebells. The rich aroma of fresh moss infused the air even though it hadn't rained for a few days, luckily. Otherwise, the trail would be slick with mud.

I came to a halt. On the edge of the trail, two enormous toadstools sprouted from the moss. They looked like tiny Smurf houses. One even had a mark on the stem that looked like a door. "Look," I said. "Three apples high."

"What?"

"Three apples high."

Dalton's blank stare made it clear he had no idea what I was talking about.

"The Smurfs. You know, little blue elves that live in the forest in tiny mushroom houses." When I was a kid, my dad would send me in search of Smurfs in the forest. Kinda like a snipe hunt, I suppose.

"Smurfs?" he said as if checking to be sure I wasn't delusional.

"It was a cartoon," I said, suddenly feeling silly. "Forget it."

About twenty minutes later, we emerged from the birches and the trail took a sudden turn upwards. I heard a strange sound, so out of place it made me stop and look around, trying to get my bearings. Then I heard it again: a metallic jangle from the trail above us. Clank-clank-clank. A billy goat.

He stopped when he saw us, tilted his head to the side, then continued toward us in that silly hoppity bounce, all four hooves springing in unison, like a toddler who's found a mud puddle. Another followed, then another, bouncy-bouncy-bouncing down the hill, braying at us.

Within moments, we were surrounded by a whole gaggle of goats, swarming, nudging, maneuvering in their skittish way. I held out my hand and five pushed and shoved to check it out. I didn't have food, but that didn't stop them. One brave goat with nubbins for horns gummed my fingers. He pulled away with a look of disappointment. *Sorry, bub.*

Another chewed at my shoelaces. I shooed him away. Goats will eat anything.

"Let's get some pictures," I said to Dalton and leaned down and put my arm around a goat. It nuzzled my cheek.

Dalton started to laugh.

"Get the shot. Get the shot," I said.

He snapped a few and bent over, cracking up. "You're a nut, you know that?"

"Yep," I said. "Deal with it."

Once the goats realized we had no food, they lost interest and meandered away, munching on grasses.

Dalton swept his arm upward with a flourish, gesturing toward the trail. "Shall we continue?"

"We shall," I said and led the way.

I had to grab hold of rock edges and small tree trunks to crawl up the steep incline. I glanced back at Dalton. He kept pace with me without any sign of complaint, as though we were taking an easy stroll on the docks. He made it look effortless. I, on the other hand, tried not to huff and puff too loudly. He'd never let me live it down.

Then all trees and bushes were behind us and the hillside was a jumble of rocks, mud, and grass. Our hike turned into genuine rock-scrambling as we clambered over boulders using hands and feet. In some of the steeper spots, rope lay across the rocks, strung there by some local trail angel. I took hold of one to help keep me steady on all fours as I climbed upward.

"Don't load it with your entire weight," Dalton said.

I nodded. I knew. We couldn't be sure how securely fastened it was at the top.

Dalton stayed right behind me, giving me the sensation that he was patiently waiting, following at my pace like you would a toddler taking her first steps. It made me want to take out his left kneecap.

Finally, I crawled over the rounded edge of the summit and could finally walk upright once again. I spun around, a full three-sixty. I could see for miles. The landscape looked like a photograph, it was so perfectly stunning. Above, blue sky stretched into forever with wisps of fluffy clouds. Below, a dark blue sea shimmered in the sunlight. The two were separated by spikes of gray blanketed in lush green.

I found a boulder, plopped down, and leaned back to take in the warm sun on my face.

Dalton sat down beside me, tipped up his water bottle, chugged down a few swallows, then offered it to me.

"I admit," he said. "I never really gave Norway much thought, but it's stunning. Just look at that."

I wiped sweat from my forehead. "Yeah, takes your breath away, doesn't it? So pristine."

"It's nice to know they appreciate it here. So many places I've been, the citizens are too busy trying to survive to think about the environment." His expression turned gray, his mind off in one of those places.

"Afghanistan, you mean?" I guzzled down some water.

"In the mornings, a mist would linger in the mountains. It made everything look soft and peaceful." He turned away as though he didn't want me to see his eyes. He absently traced his shoelaces with his fingers. "But it was more like a shroud, hanging over all the death and despair."

I looked out over the ocean, giving him space and feeling like a heel for all the times I'd given him crap about being a SEAL. He'd served his country. Honorably. I respected that. Sometime I'd drum up the nerve to tell him. Not now, though. Now wasn't the right time.

I picked up a dry leaf from the ground and rolled it between my fingers, crackling it into dry bits that fluttered to the ground. Then, hoping it had been a respectful length of time, I raised the binoculars and scanned the surface of the ocean. "I don't see any boats. Do you think we could see whales from this far away?"

"I don't know," he said, slowly coming back to me. "But

we've got all afternoon."

We sat together, under the sun, taking in the magnificent view. It was easy. Comfortable. I felt a little closer to him. He'd let me in. A tiny opening, but he'd shared something of himself with me.

"Dalton, what if she was wrong? What if he doesn't show up here? What if we can't find him?"

He gave me a warm smile. The dimple appeared again. "We'll find him."

"Yeah, but the odds—"

"We'll find him."

"How do you figure?"

He flashed a lopsided grin. "With your brains and my stunning good looks? How can we lose?"

I smiled, a full, contented smile. His optimism was contagious. And the sun was shining. And the air was fresh and clean.

"You hungry?" he asked and slipped off his daypack.

I had no idea what he'd packed and it made me a little nervous. I'm not a fan of mystery food.

He unzipped the pack and took out a tiny tarp and laid it on the ground. Then he set out a plate of grapes and cheeses, then another plate with mini-sandwiches—some with peanut butter, some bologna—another with crackers, and olives. Then another plate with hummus and veggies.

"Wow," I said, genuinely impressed. "That's quite the spread. You found all that in that tiny grocery store? How'd you even know what it was?" And he'd remembered I'm a vegetarian. Nice.

"Ah, but that's not all." He pulled from the pack a water bottle filled with red wine and two plastic stemmed glasses. He handed them to me to hold while he poured. He set down the bottle, took his glass in hand, raised it, and said, "To our new partnership."

Warmth rushed to my cheeks. *Don't turn pink. Don't turn*

pink.

His eyes locked with mine, his expression serious. "I'm sorry I gave you such a hard time in Costa Rica. It wasn't fair of me."

I nodded. I didn't know what to say. He'd already apologized.

"Onward," he said. "You and I are going to make a great team."

His eyes held mine and I was speechless under his gaze. *Just don't blush. Please don't blush.*

"I'm a lucky man."

A tingling rippled at the back of my throat and I felt the heat in my cheeks, marring my face with splotchy patches. *Damn.*

He raised his glass to his lips.

"Yes, I...me too," I stuttered, then tipped back the glass and drank down a warming swallow.

He picked up the plate with the sandwiches and held it for me to take one.

"Thank you," I said and stuffed one into my mouth, thankful for the excuse to say nothing.

He watched as I chewed, making me feel all squirmy and self-conscious. "Good?" he asked.

I nodded, then swallowed. "Yum."

Then I reached for another and in minutes we'd devoured the meal.

Dalton popped the last mini-sandwich into his mouth and licked the tips of his fingers with a flourish, then wiped them dry on his pants. "Not too bad if I do say so myself," he said with a grin. He leaned back on his elbows to relax, then sat back up with a jerk. "I almost forgot. I brought dessert."

From the pack, he offered a chocolate bar. *Chocolate!*

"Oh," I drooled. "I could kiss you."

His eyebrows shot up. "Yeah?"

"Well, you know what I mean." I snatched the bar from his hand, ripped the paper wrapper open, snapped off a square with my teeth, and mashed it around in my mouth, all the chocolaty goodness caressing my taste buds and soothing my soul. "Nom, nom, nom," I said, grinning with pleasure.

"My, my," he said. "I'd always heard chocolate was an aphrodisiac, but wow, you look like you're about to…" He let the sentence hang unfinished.

I froze, my teeth clamped together. "What?"

"Nothing." He was staring at my lips. "You've got a little…" He raised his hand as if to wipe the side of my mouth, but paused, then wiped at the corner of his own mouth. "A little chocolate." His expression seemed almost embarrassment.

I stuck out my tongue and licked the corner of my mouth.

His eyes grew wide and I burst out laughing.

He shook his head and chuckled. "You're crazy, you know that?"

I couldn't stop laughing.

"You really are something."

"What does that even mean?" I asked.

"It means…" He turned away from me, looking out at the landscape. "It means I have no idea what to do with you."

"You should trust me, that's what. If you would have trusted me in Costa Rica—"

His head jerked back in my direction, his eyes gone dark. "I said I was sorry."

I was quiet a moment. "I didn't mean…" *Dammit! Why'd I go and say that?* The silence lengthened. Finally, I got up and stretched. "We should probably head back," I said.

"Yeah."

Chapter 5

After a quiet dinner where Dalton pushed food around on his plate and stared into space for long bouts, I retreated to the cockpit to watch the evening sun turn the gray peaks into shades of pink and try once again to get interested in the paperback I had brought, some dime-store mystery I'd picked up in the airport. After that hike, I should have felt relaxed, but a nagging restlessness persisted. I hadn't meant to insult Dalton. *He just…dammit. I swear, we're like oil and water.*

I stared at the open page of the book—page 46—for about an hour.

Around eight o'clock, in the pitch dark, a fishing vessel puttered into the marina. She turned to dock and under the halogen lights, I was able to clearly see the name painted on the transom—*Forseti.*

"It's him," I whispered down the companionway to Dalton. "Ray Goldman is here."

"I'll be damned. Dr. Parker came through," he said as he climbed out of the cabin and stood beside me.

"The boat's much smaller than I'd imagined. I thought we were looking for a whaling vessel."

Dalton frowned. "I'm sure that's what the informant said, the *Forseti.*"

"Could there be two?"

"Unlikely. Usually the name has to be registered."

"How will he bring an orca aboard such a small boat? Either he's an idiot or we're missing something."

Dalton combed his fingers through his hair. "Or we've been sent on a wild goose chase."

I didn't like this revelation. I didn't like it one bit. I tried to call Dr. Parker, but there was no answer. "We need to get a look at that boat."

Dalton shook his head.

"I'm going to go see what I can find out," I said and moved to step off the boat and onto the dock.

He blocked my way. "We shouldn't be so obvious."

"What? You can't trust me to take an evening stroll on the docks?"

"That's not—" Dalton said to the back of my head as I stepped off the boat.

I halted in my tracks. *Dammit.* I'd done it again. I turned around but Dalton had already turned his back and was headed down the companionway.

I meandered toward the fuel dock where the *Forseti* had tied up. As I approached, I snuck glances at the three men who stood near the bow, talking in low whispers. One nodded over his shoulder as I walked by and said, "Well, hello there."

He was about my age, maybe a bit older. Not bad looking. His hair separated at his forehead in a perfectly placed cowlick, giving him an irresistible look of boyish-sophistication. The kind of guy I'd give a chance if he hit on me in a bar. Maybe let him talk for a while, see if there was anything worthwhile going on upstairs. His jeans fit nicely, that was sure. Snug, but not too tight. His hands were tucked into the pockets of his fleece jacket. He smiled at me and I felt all tingly. Yep. I admit. He was damn yummy.

"Oh my gosh, you're an American, aren't you?" I sighed, that silly American-girl sigh. "What are you doing in Norway?"

He turned from the other men without a word, his eyes on me, and said, "Work."

"Fishing?" *Yep, stating the obvious.*

"For now," he said. Whatever that meant. His eyes said, *It's time to play.*

"Is this your boat?" I moved toward it. If I could get him talking, I'd have an excuse to hang around, see what I could see. "She's a beauty. I've always wondered how the fish are caught with those nets and such. How does that work anyway?" I shoved my hand at him. "I'm Poppy, by the way. Here on, well, vacation I guess, if you call being on a boat a vacation. And you are?"

His smile widened. I tingled some more. "Michael."

I glanced at the other two men, but neither even looked my way or acknowledged me. They turned their shoulders toward each other, blocking me out. *Grumps.*

I took another step toward the vessel. Maybe Michael would invite me on board. "I bet you're real familiar with the surrounding area, all the inlets and coves. I was wondering about good spots to anchor, you know. Maybe you could point out a few? If you don't mind."

An older man strode down the dock and stepped between me and Michael. With a crumpled, unlit cigarette clamped between his fingers, he gestured for me to move along. "My men have work to do."

I blinked twice. It was him. Ray Goldman. In the flesh. He didn't look too menacing, clad in Carhartt overalls tucked into floppy rubber boots. In fact, with his hulking shoulders and heavy brow, he looked more like a caveman than an internationally-wanted criminal. He'd certainly passed his prime, with worn, yellowed teeth, ruddy cheeks, a nose wrought with broken blood vessels, and greasy hair, what he had left of it anyway. His skin was rough, a weathered texture from too much time in the sun or too many cigarettes or both.

He flicked open a Zippo lighter and lit the cigarette, a purposeful message—I'm done talking to you—then turned his back on me. I wanted to scold him; he was standing on the gas dock, for god's sake. Arrogant ass. Men like him made me want to scream. No, not scream. Made me glad we'd invented handcuffs. I kept my feet firmly planted for fear I'd give him a swift kick in the ass, sending him into the drink.

"Right," I said. "Sorry." I smiled at Michael. "Maybe tomorrow then?"

Michael shook his head. "We'll be setting out again before dawn."

"Oh my." I winked. "All work and no play."

His eyes widened, ever so slightly, then traveled down to my waist and back up. I had his attention.

"Well, I wish you calm seas," I said with a little wave.

As I walked away, two men passed me by, tall, thin and blond, most definitely Norwegian, heading down the dock in the direction of the *Forseti*. I glanced back to see them slow as they approached Ray. Perhaps locals Ray was hiring? But for what exactly? I couldn't stroll back that direction to eavesdrop now. Oh well.

My trip down the dock wasn't a total waste of time. I'd learned that the *Forseti* was headed back out to sea in the morning. That meant I had little time to get that Michael talking. If I had any sense of human nature whatsoever, I knew exactly where he and the crew would be tonight.

I hustled back to the *Sea Mist* to let Dalton know I was headed to the pub to see what I could find out.

"Not a good idea," he said with a shake of his head.

"Why not?"

"They're going to be suspicious of anyone. Especially anyone asking questions."

I tipped my head down, batted my eyelashes, and flashed my doe eyes. "Anyone?"

He rolled his eyes and turned his back on me.

"C'mon, Dalton. We need to gather as much information

as we can before they set out in the morning. This is our only chance. Besides—" I winked at him "—you don't think I know how to flirt with a guy without being obvious?"

He paced, his arms crossed, thinking. Then he stopped, looked me in the eyes and said, "What is it with you? It's like you've got something to prove." His hands went to his hips. "I don't disagree with you just because it's fun to argue, you know."

I stared back at him. Was that true? Did I come off like that? I admit, I did feel that I had something to prove. I wanted a permanent position in Special Ops. I had to show I was up to it, that I was a top-notch agent, the best of the best. I wasn't a former SEAL. I wasn't former law enforcement. My resumé... well, I didn't look like much on paper. Sure, I'd done all the extras I could in school, but experience is what they wanted to see. All I had was my own gumption. So, yeah, I guess I did have something to prove.

I opened my mouth to respond and he said, "You know what? You're right. Go on, do your thing."

I hesitated. "Really?"

"Yep. No one would suspect us of being agents. Not with the crap you pull. Yep, darlin', go ahead—" He winked as he crossed his arms. Was he mocking me now? "You're right. Nobody's going to see *you* coming."

I had some time before the crew of the *Forseti* would be headed to the pub and I couldn't shake whatever it was that was going on between me and Dalton. I found a bench with a view of the water and called my friend Chris. He's been my BFF since high school. We were Navy brats and our parents had the same duty stations. Now he's a flight attendant for Delta Airlines and I see him every few months or so. He's got a good heart but he almost got me fired when he showed up uninvited at my first undercover gig. I've forgiven him, especially since he helped me nail the kingpin, but I'm not sure Dalton ever will.

"Hey, Poppy-girl," he said when he picked up. "Whatsup?"

"Hey."

"What kind of trouble have you gotten yourself into now?"

"Funny," I said.

"Seriously, that was some risky action in Costa Rica. You back in the States now, safe and sound?"

"No. Came straight here." I paused. Wouldn't hurt to tell him. "I'm in Norway."

"What the hell are you doing in Norway?"

"And don't come here."

"Girl, I learned my lesson on that one." He snorted. "Besides, you're in one of the safest countries in the world. Nothing for me to worry about. What are you doing there?"

"Dalton and I are here undercover and—"

"Dalton, huh? I thought that was a one time deal."

"It was supposed to be but—"

"Buuuut?"

"Nash wanted us here. Together. I can't tell you the details."

"Okay."

The breeze had picked up, pushing ripples across the surface of the water.

"So why'd you call?" he asked.

"I don't know." I shifted the phone to my other ear. "Just haven't talked to you in a while."

"You never call just to talk. You're not that kind of girl. What's going on?"

"Well, I just wondered, I mean, you're a man and—"

"Oh, here it comes."

"Chris, I'm serious. I really need your advice right now."

"Poppy-girl, there's only one thing you need to know: he's got it bad for you."

"What? No, he's been assigned—"

"Sweetheart, I could tell. He's got it bad."

"You met him once, for like, five seconds."

"Uh, huh. And that's all it took." He made that clicking noise with his lips. "I'm telling you."

"Whatever."

"Oh and you aren't hot for him? This is Chris you're talking to."

"Yeah, well. Your radar is way off. He's my partner. That would be unprofessional."

"Uh, huh."

Silence.

"You talk to your mom lately?"

"Chris, don't start with me." My mom and I weren't exactly on speaking terms. Well, she was. I wasn't.

"She called me, asking about you, said she hasn't heard from you in months."

"New subject."

"She's worried about you. Especially this week, you know. Because of the anniversary of your dad's—"

"New subject!"

"Okay, okay." He paused a beat. "How's the love life?"

"Chris!"

"Touchy buttons today. He's gotten you that riled?"

"I gotta go."

"That was like thirty seconds. Must be a record."

I huffed. "Fine. How are things with you?"

He paused. "Yeah, I've gotta go too. Say hi to Dalton for me."

Errrrgh! I shoved the phone back into my pocket.

The village was so small, it couldn't be that hard to find the pub. I strolled toward the main street and, sure enough, there it was on the corner.

The lights were low, the decor typical of a seaside pub—paintings of old ships on the walls, brass fixtures, wood plank flooring—the kinds of items that would be made of plastic and arranged in an attempt to create an authentic atmosphere in some themed restaurant in the U.S. Here, they were the real deal. So was the odor of sea salt, weathered wood, and mildew mixed with the bitter smell of stale beer.

Music played on some old speakers and there were enough patrons to create a low roar of conversation. In the back, some men played billiards.

I scanned, looking for any of the crew I'd seen.

Bingo. In the corner sat Michael, the American man I'd met on the dock. Next to him was a Norwegian who had the look of an old salt. No doubt, he'd spent his life on the deck of a fishing vessel—crusty beard, wrinkles at the edges of his blue eyes from squinting in the sun, cheeks a permanent rose color.

On the other side of the table sat a boy who couldn't be a day over twenty, with red hair and freckles and a pair of glasses that belonged on a professor of archeology. He was so tall and gangly, he looked like he had to neatly fold his legs and arms to fit into the booth. They looked bored and restless, tired of each other's company.

I waited at the bar until Michael looked my way, then flashed him a come-hither-smile. Without a second glance, he abandoned his beer and mates and crossed the pub to greet me.

"Hi there. Poppy, was it?" He had an easy smile and soft eyes.

I nodded.

"Hey, I'm sorry my father was so gruff with you. Let me buy you a drink?"

"Sure, a drink would sooth my sorrows," I said with a wink. His Father. Michael was Ray's son. *Interesting.* I needed to be extra careful.

"He can come off as a crotchety old man, but he's really not that bad," he said. "Times have been tough and he's not thrilled about being out fishing again. Hopefully, after this trip, he can retire."

I bet. With a cold million. "Who are your friends?" I asked.

"Oh, that's the crew. Bjørn is the helmsman. Dylan's cook and deckhand."

I eyed Bjørn. Was he the informant? Damn, I should have gotten a description from Dalton.

Michael had a look on his face. I'd stared too long.

"Be-yorn?" I said to cover. "He doesn't look like a Be-yorn. Wasn't that the name of the songwriter in ABBA?"

Michael shrugged, uninterested.

"My father was into ABBA," I said, feeling as though I needed an explanation.

"Oh," he said, nodding with the fake, that's-so-interesting smile.

The front door swung open and a man strolled in, looking around with the agitation of someone who'd been called away from an expensive hooker's bed.

I drew in a breath and quickly turned away. It was the man from Bergen, the hustler in the pub. He still had the mark I'd put on his potato face. *Crap!* Five hundred miles north and here he was. *He must be the informant.* Head slap.

"I've got to talk with this guy." Michael turned away from me. "I'll have to catch you later."

I put my hand on his shoulder. "Hey, we were just getting started."

He jerked from my grip. "I said I gotta go."

Okay, geez. You don't have to be an asshole. "I'll be around," I said to the back of his head.

The informant went straight to the table with Bjørn and Dylan. Michael followed him over there, but then the two of them moved to a different table to talk. The old Norwegian, Bjørn, followed them with his eyes, his expression unreadable.

I tried not to be conspicuous while I kept a close eye on them. They leaned forward, into the table and talked in low voices. Whatever they were talking about, Michael didn't want Bjørn or Dylan to know. Then the door opened and Ray pushed through to their table. Oh, to be a fly in his beer.

Potato Head glanced around the pub, annoyed. He thrust his chair back in a huff and headed for the bar. Right next to me. *Crap.* I needed to take control of this.

"Can I get something to drink," he said to the bartender.

"What'll you have?" The man responded without looking up from the counter he was wiping with a wet rag.

He ordered some beer I'd never heard of.

"Excuse me," I asked. "Have we met before?"

He smiled and looked right at me. His smile faded and his eyeballs rattled around in his skull, searching for an escape.

I clamped my hand down on his arm and gave him a sheepish grin. "Sorry about the misunderstanding in Bergen."

He glanced over at Ray, then made an overly exaggerated examination of the contents of his wallet.

"Put it on my tab," I said to the bartender, then whispered, "I had no idea you were, well, you. You wouldn't give my partner your description. How was I supposed to know?"

From his expression, I gathered he'd like to knock my head against the bar.

He turned so his back was to Ray.

"Do you have any new information to share?" I said as quietly as I could.

"Are you kidding?" he said, rubbing his temple.

"I said I was sorry?"

His face turned a lighter shade. "Don't you know how dangerous he is?"

Dalton had been right; this guy was squirrelly. I'd be lucky if he didn't tell Ray who I was right now.

He glanced over his shoulder, fidgeted with his sleeve, then took a cigarette from a box in his pocket and clamped his thin lips around it. "I ain't sayin' nothing more."

Informants always said that, but deep down, they wanted to

blab. "How long is your little powwow gonna be? I want to get a look at that boat."

He shook his head. "No, no, no. Not a good idea. Too risky."

"I only need a few minutes." I didn't want to push him, but this was my best chance. "C'mon. Keep 'em busy?"

He eyed me up and down, making a decision, then as the bartender set his beer on the bar, he said, "And another round for my friends." He pointed to the table with one hand, grabbed his beer with the other, and left me without another word.

I downed the rest of my beer, tossed some kroner on the bar, and headed straight for the docks, a smile on my face.

The *Forseti* was a typical seine fishing vessel with the addition of a crow's nest, which was common on whaling ships. Michael had made it sound like Bjørn, Dylan, his father, and he were the entire crew. That meant no one was aboard the ship right now. I wanted to see what I could find out.

The early nightfall this time of year was a great advantage. I slinked down the dock without seeing anyone and slipped aboard. The wheelhouse might, by some chance, have information, but poking around in there was pretty risky. What I really wanted to know was how they planned to capture and transport an orca. Everything they needed must've been on deck.

There were several lazarettes, large stowage containers built into the hull. Six I could see right away. Problem was, they had big, heavy lids. If I opened one, I risked making a lot of noise. I needed to lift the lid a few inches and peek inside. But to do it one-handed while I held my phone up for a flashlight was going to be tricky.

The first was pad-locked. Not a good sign. The second had a clip in the latch. I pulled it out and heaved up the lid. Nothing but netting inside.

The next one was full of extra floats.

I turned to cross to the other side and someone grabbed me, his hand over my mouth. I rammed my elbow into his gut and spun around.

"It's me," Dalton said, wincing. "Someone's coming down the dock."

Crap.

He grabbed my hand. "We've got to hide," he said and dragged me across the deck. He lifted a pile of nets and I crawled under. He rolled in next to me and flopped the nets down on top of us. They stunk of musty, salty sea, and fish. I tried to breathe through my mouth and stay still. There was no way I was getting caught on board and blowing this op before we even got started.

"What are you doing here?" I whispered in his ear. His body was pressed tight up against me like a spoon.

He shook his head, telling me to be quiet.

Someone stepped on board, then another someone. They walked across the deck, but didn't go inside. I heard mumbling, but couldn't make out the words. Then the scratchy click-click of a cigarette lighter.

"We're going to be here for a while," I whispered to Dalton.

He nodded.

I lay there listening for any recognizable word, wondering who it was. Probably Ray. He smoked. And maybe the informant.

Dalton was warm against me. He didn't move a muscle. Not a twitch. I couldn't even tell if he was breathing. What the hell was he doing on board, anyway? Always harping on me about doing things by the book.

Finally, footsteps again. The two men moved toward the wheelhouse, then the clunk-clunk of shoes on metal stairs. Dalton rolled over. "We've got to go," he said. "Slip off at the stern and swim at least two docks over."

"What? This is the North Atlantic. Do you know how cold that water is?" Jumping into water that temperature was too risky. I wasn't sure I could do it. The shock of the cold alone could cause an automatic gasp reflex, then uncontrollable hyperventilation. Everyone in town would hear me in freak-out mode. Then, within minutes, my legs and arms would seize up. I'd sink like a stone.

"It's our best choice," he whispered.

"It's official. SEALs are insane."

Footsteps again. Someone else boarded the ship. Dalton pulled me to him and held me tight. I lay still, pressed up against him, our faces smooshed together. My heart was thrumming, but not from fear.

Whoever it was followed the others into the wheelhouse.

"C'mon, an evening dip," Dalton whispered. "Think how romantic it will be."

I elbowed him. "What are you doing here, anyway?"

"What am I doing here? What are *you* doing here?"

"Isn't this considered an illegal search? Trespassing or something?"

"Do you mean whether you do it or me?"

Good point. "Now what are we going to do?"

"Wait until they're all asleep, then slip off the back like I said."

"But once they're down below, they might hear us walking on deck." I thought a moment. Lights were on inside the wheelhouse. That meant they couldn't see in the darkness outside. "I'm taking the dock." I rolled from under the nets and took off crab-crawling across the deck before he could grab me.

"Dammit, Poppy," he said in a whisper yell, but he was right behind me.

I poked my head over the rail. "Coast is clear," I said and leaped over the side and onto the dock.

Dalton appeared beside me. He took my hand in his and

we sauntered down the dock like any other tourists out for an evening stroll.

As we neared our boat, a couple sailors appeared out of the darkness, walking toward us. Dalton put his arm around me and whispered in my ear. "That was risky, McVie."

I leaned into him, my head on his shoulder. "You smell like fish."

Chapter 6

It was still pitch dark at six a.m. when Dalton fired up the engine. I shuffled around the deck, careful not to trip over any lines or a cleat.

Dalton helped untie the lines and we cast off.

The vessel came equipped with a hand-held spotlight. I stood on the bow, shining a path through the marina while Dalton steered past the fishing docks.

The *Forseti* was still docked, but we wanted to get out of the harbor first. That way, they wouldn't think we were following them.

Once we were past the break wall and out in open water, we could relax a bit. I gazed up at the night sky. Stars spread across the heavens, sparkling like sequins on a royal blue evening gown. The air was cool and crisp. The water calm. The *Sea Mist* gently pushed through the current leaving a tiny white line of froth on the black surface of the sea.

I joined Dalton in the cockpit. "How does she handle?" I asked.

"Like a dream."

"I'm glad you won the coin toss," I said with a grin. "I'd prefer to take the helm when we've hoisted the sails anyway."

"For now, we play cat and mouse. We keep the *Forseti* in our sights while looking like incompetent tourists."

"I don't know about you, but I could use some coffee."

"I won Captain for the day. That makes you the galley wench, right?"

"Don't push your luck," I said and slipped down the companionway.

I found a percolator pot in a bin, filled it with water and coffee, clamped it onto the stovetop, and fired up the burner. Within minutes the aroma of fresh coffee filled the cabin. Dalton poked his head down the hatch. "A fine galley wench you are, mate. My mouth is watering up here."

I found a couple thermal mugs and joined Dalton on deck with the fresh brew.

To the east, the horizon glowed orange. The clouds above looked rimmed with fire.

Dalton had chosen a location where we could safely drift, waiting for the *Forseti*.

I kicked back and sipped my coffee. "There are worse jobs," I said.

"Don't I know it," Dalton said with a grin. He let the engine idle.

"I hope this isn't a waste of time."

He shrugged. "Time on the ocean, fresh air, a sunrise, just the two of us. How could it be a waste of time?"

"You know what I mean."

"There's no wind. Perhaps we should hoist the sails until we determine which way he's headed. We'll look like amateurs caught in irons."

"No time. Look." A fishing vessel was rounding the breakwater. "I bet that's them." I raised the binoculars to check the number on her bow. "It's the *Forseti*."

Dalton took hold of the throttle and eased the boat into gear. "Any indication to which way they're heading?"

I shook my head. "Can't tell."

If the *Forseti* headed southwest, it meant Ray was headed around the peninsula into the open ocean. To the northeast was miles of fjords leading into smaller, narrower fjords. His choice would tell us if he had up-to-date information as to where the killer whales would be.

I raised the binoculars again. "South," I said. "He's turning south."

Dalton turned the wheel to match the heading of the *Forseti* and gave her a little more throttle.

"What do you think, my darling Brittany? Shall we go sightseeing? Maybe some whale watching?"

I nodded. "The cameras are ready." I paused. "But please don't call me Brittany. I left that moniker in Costa Rica." *That and having to play your ditsy wife.* That hadn't worked out so well. "From now on, I'm Poppy."

We followed the coastline for what seemed the entire length of Norway, but was more like twenty miles or so. Puttering along at six knots, the scenery goes by awfully slowly, as stunning as it is. But I'd never get bored.

That's what my mother didn't get, what she never gets. Not like my dad. When we set sail that summer when I was a kid, he knew I'd take to it like a true adventurer. That was my first taste of absolute freedom. We had the whole world to explore.

If only our trip hadn't been cut short.

The day had been like any other, though the wind had shifted from a constant, gentle, westerly wind, to a southerly, twenty-knot blow. We were running downwind, the breeze at our backs. My father, always the patient teacher, had explained the points of sail, the techniques and maneuvers, and I was anxious to learn. My job was to man the sheets. I'd let them out or pull them in using the winch, depending on my dad's commands.

What I didn't realize then, was that he had learned pretty much all he knew about sailing from reading *Chapman's*, the bible of sailors. He had no practical experience. But he'd warned me about the danger of an accidental jibe when sailing downwind like we were, how the wind could catch the outside of the mainsail and send the boom whipping across the boat and slamming against the lines on the other side.

"You're awfully quiet," Dalton said, interrupting my memories.

I nodded. "Thinking about that summer with my dad."

"Want to tell me about it?"

"There's not much to tell." I looked at Dalton. His expression was earnest. *What the hell. Why not?* "Except this one story."

"I could use a good story," he said, his smile kind.

"My dad and I, well, we weren't exactly seasoned sailors and then this one day—well, we'd practiced the jibe many times. My dad would handle the sheets, so he could control the boom as it crossed the deck. I loved it because I got to take the helm—"

"Well, that certainly hasn't changed," Dalton said, his eyes teasing.

"Do you want to hear the story or not?"

He made like he was zipping his lips.

"That day, I stood on the bow looking for wildlife. Not three days earlier, I'd spotted a pod of humpback whales, the first I'd ever seen, and all I could think about was spotting more of them."

I'd seen dolphins quite often, playing at the bow. Seals and sea lions, even a couple otters, had bid us hello.

"Something caught my eye. To this day, I couldn't say for sure what it was, but at the time I was convinced it was an injured otter."

Dalton was nodding, but now I wasn't sure I wanted to tell him about it.

Just thinking about my dad made my eyes get all misty.

The thing is, it all started with my need to help a hurt animal.

I had hollered to my father, pointing at the water. "It's hurt, Daddy, I'm sure!" I shouted. "Turn around."

He leaned from the helm, looking over his shoulder. "What is it?" he hollered back. He leaned a bit further. Then it happened. The boat shifted. Ever so slightly. The wind caught the back of the sail and the boom swept across the deck and slammed into my dad's head, knocking him down. He collapsed in the cockpit, slumped against the wheel.

Blood gushed from his forehead, his neck turned at an unnatural angle. I rushed across the deck. "Daddy! Daddy!" He was out cold. I felt the boat start to shift again and I ducked as the boom came whipping back across, shaking the boat as it slammed to the end of the lines.

I had to get control of the helm before I could take care of my dad.

I spun the wheel to tack through the wind, leaving the jibsheet secured on the cleat, and let the mainsail flutter, trying to get the boat to heave to. We hadn't practiced the maneuver and I had to do it twice to get the boat to settle, but when I was sure it had, I lashed the wheel to lock the rudder, and we floated with the waves, the boat steady.

"Wake up, Daddy! Wake up!" He didn't respond.

I rushed down below for the first aid kit. With a mound of gauze, I stopped the bleeding on his head, but I knew a concussion was much more serious. I got on the radio and called out the emergency code, "Pan-pan, Pan-pan, Pan-pan."

The U.S. Coast Guard replied, asking me to explain my emergency.

"My dad's knocked out cold by the boom," I said, my voice shaking.

"Okay," the man came back. "Is it just you two on board?"

"Yes."

"Okay. I'm going to help. What's your name and how old are you?"

"I'm Poppy. I'm twelve."

There was a long pause.

"I've got the boat hove to and I've bandaged his head, but…" I tried not to cry. "But he's not waking up."

"Okay, Poppy. I'm going to send someone right away to help you. But I need you to tell me where you are. I need your coordinates, if you can. Does your dad have any electronic—"

"No, we don't have GPS," I said.

"All right," he said. "Do you remember what port you left from and how long ago that was?"

"Well, yeah, but don't you want to know exactly where we are?"

"Yes, Poppy, that's what I'm trying—"

"Hold on." I flew down the ladder and grabbed the chart. Whenever my dad and I traveled, I was in charge of navigating. I'd been plotting our course, keeping watch on the coastline, our speed and direction, marking our progress with a pencil every hour. I checked the clock, used the ruler, and quickly scribbled down our current longitude and latitude. I raced back up the ladder. Dad was still out cold. Into the radio, I rattled off the coordinates.

"Are you sure that's your location?"

"Yes, sir," I said. "I'm the navigator."

"Okay, okay," he said. "I'm sending help right now. A helicopter to take your dad to a doctor."

"Well, tell them to hurry," I said.

"I will," he said and I could tell he was suppressing that disparaging, isn't-she-cute-chuckle. "I want you to stay on the radio and talk to me, though, okay."

"Why? Don't you have work to do?"

Another long pause.

"Yes, Poppy. This is my job. To make sure you and your dad are all right, to be right here to talk you through everything while others come in the helicopter. Is your dad still asleep?"

I looked over at him and tears bubbled up in my eyeballs. "Yes."

"Okay, everything's going to be okay."

"He's getting sunburned."

"What? What do you mean?"

"The sun. I don't know if he put on sunscreen today. He's like me. We have to be careful in the sun. It's the red hair,"

"It's all right, Poppy. The helicopter will be there soon. Listen to me, Poppy. Do you know how to sail the boat?"

"Yes. Of course," I said.

"Okay, then." He asked me a bunch of questions about the boat, about my dad, where we were from. He even asked where was my mom. I told him she was in the Navy. After awhile, I realized he was trying to keep me talking.

My dad moved, shifting a little. He groaned and blinked open his eyes.

"Daddy, are you okay, Daddy?"

He squinted in the sun. "What the hell?"

Tears showered down my face, stinging my sunburned cheeks. "You got hit by the boom."

He rubbed his head and the mound of gauze I'd taped there. "Did you…?" His eyes traveled to the sails, then to the wheel. "What happened?"

"It's okay. The Coast Guard is coming."

"I don't need—"

"My dad's awake," I said into the radio.

"Good, Poppy. Now look south. Do you see the helicopter? It's almost there."

"I see it." The orange aircraft was flying low, headed right for us.

My dad looked up, then leaned over and threw up on the floor. Then he leaned back and passed out again.

"He's sick. My dad is sick."

"Did he vomit? That's okay. He's probably feeling a little dizzy and it's nothing to worry…"

The roar of the helicopter drowned out his voice. It slowed and hovered overhead, so loud I had to cover my ears. The blades whipped the water into a mist. Then the rescue swimmer jumped from the helicopter into the water beside the sailboat. I thought Superman had arrived, I swear.

Once he was in the water, the helicopter flew up and away. Not too far, just enough so I could hear the man talk. I helped him get on board. I'll never forget his name. Petty Officer Jon Ardan. He kept asking if I was okay. I nodded like crazy.

"Are you okay?" Dalton was saying, bringing me back to today. He stared at me with expectant eyes. "You were saying you saw an otter in the water, then your eyes glazed over."

"Yeah, I thought I saw an otter. My dad turned, the wind caught the sail, and he got hit by the boom. Knocked him out cold."

"Wow, that's serious. What'd you do?"

"I called the Coast Guard. They came."

"That's it? That's your whole story?"

"Pretty much. When they got there,—" I pressed my lips together, wincing at the memory "—'Help my dad,' was all I could say through my blubbering."

Dalton gave me a sympathetic smile. "Poppy, you were twelve."

"Yeah, well…"

The helicopter had circled back and a huge basket was lowered on the cable. Petty Officer Ardan strapped my dad onto a litter in the basket, then I watched, powerless to help, as my dad was brought up into the helicopter and it flew away, leaving the petty officer on board with me.

"It's funny," I said to Dalton. "I remember…"

"What?"

I turned away from Dalton and gazed out at the horizon. "Nothing."

I remember staring at the petty officer, in his jumpsuit, a real superhero, and it hit me that my dad was just a man. An ordinary man.

"So your dad, was he okay?" Dalton asked.

"Yeah."

They had kept my dad overnight and I got to sleep on a little pull-out-couch in his room.

In the morning, he opened his eyes and smiled at me. "My hero," he said.

I shook my head. He took my hand in his and I started to shake, then my eyes filled with tears and I buried my head in his chest. "Oh Daddy, I thought you were going to die."

"Now how could that be? With you there to take care of me?"

I shook my head, snuffling.

"Did you remember what I taught you? About breathing?"

I nodded. He'd shown me how to control my heart rate, to keep from panicking, by controlling my breath.

"It's important to always practice the pranayama. Your breath is your life force, the vital energy we share with all life."

I nodded again. I drew in a deep breath and felt better.

Then my mom arrived. "What were you thinking? I knew something like this would happen," she said to him before he could sit up in the bed. She was still in her uniform and her eyes were red. She must have flown through the night. I remember thinking, that must be why they call it the red eye.

My dad held his head in his hands. "Georgia, calm down. Everything turned out all right."

"But she was on her own. What if you'd have fallen off the boat? Where would she be, a twelve-year-old, trying to rescue you on her own?"

"She'd be further ahead than most twelve-year-olds, that's where, because she'd have done it."

My mother got that look on her face, the one that said, *don't you dare say another word.* She crossed her arms. "This trip is over."

"What!" I shot up from the chair.

She almost bowled me over with a bear hug. "Oh my dear. Are you okay?"

"Why does everyone keep asking me if I'm okay? It was Dad who got hurt, not me."

"You must have been terrified." She rocked me, rubbing my back.

I tried to pull away. "Well, I really didn't..." I'd learned not to confirm anything my mom said. She'd turn it around on me.

"We're going to get your things and you're coming back to the base with me."

"But Mom, I'm not—"

"No buts. Now get your things."

And that was that. Mom had brought down her fist and our sailing trip was over. She enrolled me in school and my dad decided to go off on a photography trip on his own.

Dalton took hold of my hand. "Your hand is shaking."

"I'm fine." I turned away. I couldn't look at him. "That was the last time I saw my dad, is all."

"Poppy, don't be too hard on yourself. You were just a kid."

I pulled my hand from his. "Yeah," I said and escaped to the cabin below.

When I got back topside, Dalton was at the helm, one arm draped over the top of the wheel, the other holding his cup of coffee, his hair ruffled in the wind. He seemed at ease, content. I couldn't help but stare a moment. If he wasn't so damn aggravating, I might have found him attractive. He was an adrenaline junkie like me. Bold and confident. And he had the looks—that strong jaw line, the way he held his shoulders, how every muscle formed to create a body that Michelangelo's *David* would envy.

Yeah, no. He was so damn aggravating.

I forced my eyes forward, to the edge of the sea, and my mind somewhere else.

Around lunch time, the *Forseti* overtook us.

"I hope this all happens and is done quickly," I said. "I don't think they'll tolerate us for long."

Dalton said nothing but I could tell by his expression that he had the same concern.

In the galley, I flipped some lunchmeat and mustard on a slice of bread for Dalton, some peanut butter for me and we kept moving.

When I handed him his sandwich, he asked, "So after that summer, sailing with your dad, that's when he was killed, by poachers, right?"

"Yeah," I said.

"What happened?"

I shrugged. I didn't want to talk about it. This time every year, the date of my dad's death, always refueled my anger and frustration. I didn't like the conclusions of the authorities. Never would. They'd dismissed it too easily. They didn't know my dad like I did. Someday. Someday I'd track down the culprits and justice would be done.

"I'm sorry," Dalton said. I wasn't sure if he meant for losing my dad or for bringing it up.

I shrugged again. "How's the sandwich?"

"Great, thank you," he said, taking the hint.

Sometime in the late afternoon, the *Forseti* slowed and turned into a small inlet. It looked like they meant to anchor.

"I figured they'd press on through the night," Dalton said. "Didn't you say Dr. Parker's last text said that the whales are still quite far out?"

"Maybe they know something we don't?"

Dalton continued another mile to a nice, secluded cove and we dropped anchor. We had to assume they'd continue in the morning. "I don't like this," I said. "Do you suppose they got word there are other killer whales close by? A pod Dr. Parker doesn't have tagged? And they're going after them instead?"

He scanned the ocean with the binoculars. "We should get some rest while we can. We'll take shifts."

"You've been at the helm all day. You go ahead," I said. "I'll wake you in four hours."

"You'll wake me if anything else comes up though, right?" he said. "You're not going to take off in the dingy on your own for some clandestine nighttime assault, right?"

I crossed my arms.

"Right," he said and grabbed the handrails and swung into the companionway.

I shook my head. *That man.*

The cockpit wasn't the most comfortable for lounging, but I managed to prop up a cushion and face the open sea. I once again opened my book, but I wasn't in the mood. It wasn't very often I got to watch the sunset on a sailboat anchored at sea. In fact, a glass of wine seemed appropriate. I slipped down below, found a plastic mug, and filled it with Cabernet from a box. (On a boat, it would do.) *Ah.*

I settled into the cushions and thought of calling Chris back, but I didn't want Dalton to hear my conversation. I'd been snippy with him and he was just trying to be my friend. It was the mention of my mom. Always put me on edge. I sighed. He'd understand.

The sea was calm as glass, the reflections of the surrounding peaks a perfect mirror image. The kak-kak of sea birds mingled with the babble of distant waterfalls. I sipped my wine. *Sure beats lying in the mud in a blind swatting mosquitoes and hoping the poachers don't have itchy trigger fingers.*

A faint soothing sound broke the quiet. I grabbed the binoculars and as I lifted them to see, I heard it again—the distinctive whoosh of a humpback whale exhaling as it broke the surface. I stood up. There were three, no four. Maybe five. About a half mile out. And they were headed toward us.

I stood in awe, watching as the group surfaced for air three more times, their warm breath held aloft in tiny clouds of mist. Then on the fifth exhalation, each arched its back and as it dove, showed its distinctive fluke.

I zinged down the ladder. "Dalton, wake up. Wake up."

He sat up with a jolt. "What is it? What's wrong?"

He rubbed his eyes and ran his fingers through his hair, sitting on the edge of the bunk, shirtless and wearing only his boxer shorts. For a moment, I forgot what I'd come down for. "Nothing," I said and forced my eyes to the floor. His shoes had been placed next to the bunk in perfect alignment atop his shirt and jeans, folded with perfect corners and stacked one atop the other. "Come see," I said, louder than I intended to as I backed out of his cabin.

We got top side as one of the whales surfaced again, this time within two hundred yards. It exhaled and water sprayed into the air with a resounding whoosh, the wistful whisper of a giant.

In moments, another surfaced, then another, their exhalations without hurry, a peaceful yogic breath, and I was reminded of the pranayama. I drew in a long breath and exhaled, concentrating on an easy, constant letting go. Just me and the water and the sky and the whales. Nothing else mattered. Then the first arched his back and as he dove, his fluke broke the surface and water poured off, separating into countless tiny streams as the tail flattened then tipped upward and slowly disappeared below the water.

As though choreographed by some ancient force, each followed in the same manner, showing us their wide tail flukes.

I turned to Dalton. "I thought you'd want to see."

He nodded, his smile wide. "Yes, thanks. And keep an eye out. Orcas often travel with humpbacks. Or the other way around. Both take advantage of the others' fishing techniques."

A whale surfaced right next to the boat, its exhalation so loud I fell back on my butt with a start. Dalton let out a whoop and I giggled. I couldn't help myself. I giggled with delight as I ran to the bow. The whale passed below in the crystal clear water, then came up on the other side and blew out a breath. The mist sprayed me in the face. "That's amazing!" My whole body tingled with joy. "Fish breath!" I said to Dalton and giggled some more.

Dalton's smile said it all.

The other humpbacks surfaced about fifty yards off the starboard bow, circling back.

"How could anyone want to harm such beautiful creatures?" I whispered.

He shook his head.

"They're just so beautiful," I said.

Dalton turned to face me. I could feel his eyes on me.

I met his gaze and his eyes held mine. Whoosh, came another watery breath. "We should take some pictures," I said and hurried down below for the camera, escaping from Dalton's gaze. I stopped and drew in a deep breath. *Don't go there, McVie. It's dangerous territory.* I got the camera and headed back topside.

I managed to snap a few frames but the whales were quickly getting further and further away. "It's amazing how much distance they cover and it feels like they're moving so slowly."

"Yeah," he muttered. "I should hit the sack again." I could tell his mind was elsewhere. "Wake me in four." He headed down below without looking at me.

CHAPTER 7

On Dalton's watch, sometime around three a.m., an easterly wind brought waves rolling into our cove. I awoke to the rhythmic rocking of our boat. Then the rain came. First a patter on the deck, then the angry pounding of a thousand tiny hammers.

I donned my boots and jacket and started to head up the companionway to ask Dalton if he was all right, but thought better of it. He'd just give me that I-was-a-SEAL frown.

Neither of us were going to get any sleep anyway, so I fired up the stove and set the coffee pot to brew. I filled it only half full as the boat bobbed and rocked in the sea. Otherwise, I'd have a black mess to clean up.

A decent breakfast wasn't going to happen. Yogurt and a banana would have to do.

As I managed to get steaming hot coffee into the mugs without splashing it all over the place, the boat rose upward on a swell and the anchor broke loose. Dalton fired up the engine immediately. I secured the coffee mugs, flipped on the navigation lights, and clipped on my life jacket before I ran up top.

"I've got the helm!" I shouted over the thunderous rain as I took the wheel.

Dalton didn't hesitate. He headed for the foredeck, hand over hand along the rail, trying to stay upright as the bow rose and fell on the waves. He started hauling in the anchor.

"You're not clipped onto the jackline!" I yelled but he couldn't hear me. If he fell overboard right now, in the pitch dark, I didn't know how I'd find him. But he had to get the anchor up as soon as possible. We'd be in serious danger if it wrapped around the prop. And he had to pull it up without letting it slam into the side of the hull.

I kept her steady as best I could, aiming into the growing swells.

Finally, he had the anchor on board and secured on the bow roller. He headed back to the mainsail, walking with the wide stance of a seasoned sailor to keep his balance while the deck moved below his feet. He pulled off the sail ties and tossed them in the cockpit, put a reef in the sail, then went right to the halyard to hoist the mainsail to stabilize the boat so we'd stop bobbing around like a lost cork. "Head to wind!" he shouted. "Head to wind!"

"I'm trying!" I needed to keep her bow into the wind, so the sail wouldn't fill as he was raising it, but the waves were too big for the 45-horsepower engine to keep her steady.

The bow swung to starboard. I forced the wheel around and pushed the throttle down, managing to get her headed into the wind. The bow pointed up on the crest of a wave, then slammed down into the trough. As she tilted upward again, water crashed over the bow and sprayed me smack in the face, the cold a shocking jolt.

My feet were braced and I held her steady into the wind as Dalton cranked the winch double-time, hoisting the sail. The moment he cleated the halyard, I turned the wheel, bearing away. The sail filled with wind, and the side-to-side bobbing subsided. The boat eased into the rhythm of her design, pitching fore and aft as she cut through the waves.

Dalton plopped down on the cockpit seat. He was soaking wet, his hair sticking to his forehead.

"That was hairy for a moment," I said.

He nodded, wiping the back of his hand across his brow.

"We should get into our harnesses before raising the headsail. This looks like it might pick up," I said.

"I'll get 'em," he said and headed down the ladder, shaking his head, mumbling, "There was nothing forecasted."

"There's coffee," I hollered after him. "I already poured it. Mugs are cinched in the sink."

He poked his head back up and grinned. "You make a great wife, you know that."

If I'd had something to throw at him, I would have.

I licked sea salt from my lips.

The halyard rattled against the mast, a metallic bang bang bang. I wanted to tighten it down, but it wasn't worth risking a walk on the deck.

Dalton appeared with coffee and our harnesses. I got into mine and clipped the tether to the jackline.

"I feel like a dog on a leash," I said.

"Maybe it will tame you," he said with a smirk.

A gust came up and the boat lifted, heeling to port. "Never!" I said to Dalton as I tightened my grip on the wheel, holding her steady.

He shook his head. "I say we use the stormsail up front. What do you think?"

I nodded. "It's really going to blow." The steel-wire stays that held the mast in place hummed, vibrating in the wind. "I'm setting a course for Reine. Back to the harbor." I adjusted the mainsail angle by easing out the mainsheet. "We're going to be rocking and rolling."

Dalton made no response as he went to work unfurling the headsail while I managed the helm. The boat picked up speed right away.

I took a quick sip of the coffee. Warmth filled my chest.

There was nothing ahead but an inky-black sea with only a hint of white lace at the tip of a wave as it curled and ran alongside the boat. Ideally, sailing at night, I'd have a lookout on the bow, but it was too dangerous in these waves.

Another gust slammed into the sails. I shifted my weight to keep my balance. The wind was picking up and we had miles to go to get back to safe harbor.

"Make sure the companionway's sealed tight," I said to Dalton. He grabbed hold of the sliding hatch and gave it a tug.

The boat rocked to starboard as a roller wave lifted, then we rocked to port as we slid into the trough. The next roller was even bigger and crashed over the starboard side sending a wave of water down the deck and splashing into the cockpit. My right boot filled with icy-cold water. Every muscle in my body tensed with the chill.

"With these gusts, I need you to mind the mainsheet," I said to Dalton.

"Yes, ma'am," he said and took hold of the line.

The wind blew so hard, the rain swept horizontally, whipping at my face under the bimini top.

The bow slammed into a wave and I lost my balance. I grabbed for the lifeline and managed to keep upright as the bow broke through and we rode up the wave.

Another wall of water rolled over the deck and poured into the cockpit, over the top of my boots.

Up then down, up and down, she rolled right, then left.

"I see light ahead," said Dalton. "Off the starboard bow, at two o'clock. Could be the *Forseti.*"

"I see it." If we could keep up with him, at least he'd be close by if we needed to radio for help.

Lightning zig-zagged across the sky, an instant of illumination, a contrast to the black, ominous waves that churned the surface of the sea.

Take 'em one at a time, Poppy. One at a time.

The size and duration of the waves was getting dangerous. With each crest, the bow dipped and slammed into the trough. The mast rattled and shook. The stays flexed, then pulled taut with each wave. I was starting to wonder if the *Sea Mist* could take it.

"We might want to have our satellite beacon at the ready," I shouted to Dalton.

"Where is it?" he said.

"Take the helm." I knew where it was stashed.

Dalton and I managed to move past each other, sloshing through the cockpit, always one hand on a rail. He grabbed the wheel and I headed down the ladder, a puddle of water forming before I could get the companionway hatch closed.

The cabin looked as though a tornado had thundered through. Cabinets doors had flung open, boxes of cereal, bags of pasta and chips scattered all over the floor. I managed to hobble to the equipment locker, moving from one handhold to another as the floor lifted and dropped. With the lid clipped open and my hip wedged against the bulkhead, I rummaged through and found the beacon. I pinned it to my life vest.

I really had to pee, but I wasn't sure I could get into the head. The door had come unlatched and was slamming open and shut with every rocking back and forth of the boat. I tried to get it latched again and decided I might as well go while I was down here. Climbing up and down the ladder wasn't exactly a safe endeavor in a storm like this.

One might think a twenty-four-year old woman could handle a potty break without incident, but on a sailboat in the high seas, well, let's just say that accidentally peeing in your own boot isn't exactly something to be criticized. Once you let loose, there's no turning back.

I braced myself against the bulkhead to get my pants buttoned back up, then tackled the ladder.

When I got back top side, the eastern sky had patches of pink light amid dark clouds. The sea looked as dark as ever. I glanced forward. The lights of the *Forseti* appeared, then disappeared behind the crest of a wave, then appeared again.

"They're gaining distance from us," Dalton said. "We can't

keep up with them."

"We need a bigger boat."

For the first time, I saw an expression of worry cross Dalton's face. There and gone. A ghost passing through, then banished.

"I don't suppose you brewed some more coffee while you were down there?" Before I could answer, he grinned and said, "I'm kidding. I think this blow is just getting started."

I nodded as I took the helm. I was afraid of the same thing.

Each wave seemed larger than the last. The swells were increasing and the *Sea Mist* rolled and rocked, tossed on the sea like a bath toy of the gods. Dalton and I held on in a constant deluge. The cockpit drain could barely keep up and soon we stood in knee deep water.

With a jolt, an exceptionally large roller crashed over the bow, surged across the deck and slammed into the cockpit, drenching us. "Whew!" shouted Dalton. "Makes you feel alive, don't it!"

"Absolutely!" I shouted back, gripping the wheel.

I glanced at the chart plotter. We'd been steadily blowing in toward shore. We needed to turn and head out, away from shore. "We need to tack," I said.

Dalton immediately got on the jib sheet.

"Ready about?" I shouted. "Helms-a-lee." I turned into the wind and released the port jibsheet. The headsail flapped and fluttered, then bent against the forestay. Dalton cranked on the winch in a frenzied hurry, tightening down the sheet as we bobbed to and fro. The mainsail boom came around, both sails filled with wind, and the boat heeled over to starboard. "We'll stay close-hauled to get away from the shore," I told him. "So hang on!"

The boat leaned so far over I had to grab hold of the rail.

With the force of the waves and the angle of heel, our forward momentum stalled.

"We need to reef the sail again," he said.

I shook my head. Not a good idea.

"We need to reef. We've got too much sail."

"I know what reef means. It's too risky to walk up on the deck right now to do it."

"I can do it," said Dalton. "Keep her steady."

"No. I'll bear away. We'll take the longer course."

"No, I can do it!"

He took three steps and slipped and fell down the side deck into the life lines. As if it were a mere stumble, he got back to his feet and continued. A monster wave crested in front of us and tumbled over the bow, thundered down the deck, and swiped his feet out from under him. He slammed into the lifelines and fell over the side.

The jackline pulled taut as he came to the end of the tether. "Dalton!" I screamed.

I turned into the wind, let the mainsheet loose, and ran to the railing. Dalton was hanging over the side, both hands on his tether, trying to haul himself back on board as waves battered him, crashing over his head.

Think! Quick! The boom slammed back and forth over my head. I grabbed the spare halyard line, wrapped it on the winch, and tossed the bitter end to Dalton. "Grab the line!" I shouted.

He tried to catch it with one hand as it flapped in the wind and water. As soon as he had a grip on it, I cranked the winch in double-time, hauling him back to the rail. He heaved himself over the lifelines and flopped into the cockpit. Dalton bent over, his head in his hands, trying to catch his breath. "Holy crap! That was quick thinking, McVie." He nodded, his way of praise.

"Just what we needed, a little excitement. It was getting boring," I said as set the mainsail and adjusted our heading.

He smiled wide, threw his head back, and let loose a hearty laugh.

Inside, my heart hammered away at my ribs. I checked the instruments and reassessed our course. "We drifted quite a bit, lost some ground. We'll have to stay on this tack for a while."

He nodded, then turned and stared at the sunrise for a long moment. "I thought I was going to have to cut loose. I was reaching for my KA-BAR." He turned back to face me. "Then there you were, with a lifeline."

"You'd do the same for me."

"Yeah, but…"

"If you'd have had to cut loose, I would've found you."

He looked me in the eyes. "No doubt you would have."

"It wouldn't look good on my resume, losing a new partner so soon."

He laughed again. "I'm sure you're right." He shook his head and turned away.

The gale blew all day, waves growing larger by the hour in the gray, dreary sea. By mid-day, we were exhausted, but we still had miles to go. We'd long since lost sight of the *Forseti*. Dalton and I took turns at the helm while the other manned the sheets, a steady mind-numbing routine punctured occasionally by moments of panic.

The cockpit never quite cleared of water and my feet were raw from cold, wet boots. My stomach growled but food didn't sound good. Besides, heading down below to get anything would be an adventure all its own.

The radio squawked to life—*Sea Mist, Sea Mist, Sea Mist*. The charter company trying to hail us. Dalton answered, told them we were en route to the harbor and our coordinates. By the time we got back to port, she'd need some repairs, he told them.

"Glad you are headed back," the man said. "The gale's supposed to blow for another couple days."

Dalton signed off and looked at me. "I hope the *Forseti* is back in port, too. Or we might never find him again."

The afternoon dragged on as the *Sea Mist* got pummeled by

wind and waves. Dalton and I held on.

By dusk, the harbor was in sight.

Once we had her back in the berth and tied up, Dalton wrapped his arms around me in a big bear hug. "We made it," he said.

"Yes, but what if the *Forseti* isn't here? What will we do then?"

Dalton combed his fingers through his hair. "My god, Girl. Take a breath."

CHAPTER 8

After a quick stroll, and finding the *Forseti* in the marina, I collapsed in my bunk.

Even in the protected harbor, the boat rocked and jerked against the lines all night. I tossed in my bed, too exhausted to sleep.

When daylight finally streamed in through the port light, I roused and set a pot of coffee to brew, then went up on deck to see if there was any movement on the *Forseti*. No sign of anyone.

Waves crashed into the breakwall and splashed twenty feet into the air, then poured over the back side. Flags fluttered at the tops of their poles. Halyards and stays rattled and hummed in the wind as boats rocked and shifted in their berths.

Back down below, I checked the weather forecast. Marine warnings darted across the screen. As we'd been told, the storm was expected to blow for another day at least, maybe more, before settling down. Thirty-foot seas and sustained forty-knot winds with gusts as high as fifty-five. No one was going anywhere.

I found a frying pan and cracked some eggs into it.

This plan wasn't going to work. We couldn't keep up with the *Forseti*, even in calm seas. There had to be another way. A better way.

I had to get on that boat.

Dalton stuck his head out of his cabin, one eye open. "Is that coffee I smell?"

"Nectar of the gods," I said. "Coming right up."

He slumped into a seat at the table. I set a mug down in front of him, trying to keep my eyes from his muscled arms and rock-hard pecs. The eggs were done, so I slid them onto a couple of plates and plopped them on the table. "Eat up," I said.

"Wow," he said. "She saves me from Neptune's mighty grip and cooks me breakfast."

"Yeah, well, don't get used to it."

I slid a fork across the table to him.

He wolfed down his eggs and chased them with two gulps of coffee.

"The *Forseti* is at the dock. I haven't seen any movement over there this morning."

"Morning? It's nearly eleven-thirty."

I glanced at the clock. He was right. I must have been more exhausted than I'd thought. I never slept this late.

"I suppose we should check in," he said and reached for his phone.

I shoved the plates in the sink. "I cooked. You clean up."

He grumbled some kind of confirmation as he scrolled through emails on his phone. "I got a note from Nash," he said. "Listen to this. He called Norwegian officials to give them a heads up and discuss arrangements, assuming we'd be successful in our mission, and it sounds like they weren't too keen on us being here. Some political crap about jurisdiction and the U.S. overstepping." He looked up at me. "The Op's been nixed. He wants us to head home right away."

"What?" I couldn't believe what I was hearing. "But what about Ray? What about the whales he'll capture?"

Dalton shrugged. "Nothing we can do if they won't have us here."

"Nothing we can do?" I plopped down on the bench across

from him. "But we can't just—"

"Poppy, I know you're—"

"You're damn right. I'm not going anywhere. Not while that man is here capturing whales. What about April? What about that pod? What about Granny K?"

"We knew this was a long shot at best coming in. Joe was going out on a limb sending us here in the first place. We don't have—"

"You write back and you tell him I'm already on the boat."

"What?" He shook his head, his jaw muscles taut. "No way. I'm not going to do that. You're not—"

"You tell him I found a way on the boat and you can't leave me without backup. Tell him there's no way to get word to me or to get me off the boat without risking my life. You tell him." I nodded emphatically. "I'm already on that boat."

"Poppy, no. No way. It's too dangerous. Besides, that is not even remotely an option. There's no way Ray is going to let a stranger on that boat. What you're thinking is impossible."

I crossed my arms. "Nothing's impossible."

Dalton stared at me, then sighed, closed his eyes. "And what exactly is your plan?"

"Well, I'll...I'm going to...I'll find a way."

He shook his head. "Poppy, you're not—"

"I'll get a job with him. I'll stowaway. I don't know." *Breathe. Breathe.* "But I am not walking away from this. I'm not. Not if I can stop it."

His eyes grew large. "Who said anything about stopping it?"

I gritted my teeth. Sure a video might be the evidence we needed to convict Ray, assuming we could convince the Norwegian authorities to take him into custody, but what good was it to the killer whale who, by then, would've already been sold into slavery and living in a bathtub in Russia or China? Of course I had to stop it.

I mustered calm. "I'm doing this. Are you with me or not?"

He stared at me, his eyes filled with apprehension, then he examined the inside of his coffee mug for a while, then finally looked back at me, shaking his head. "This is a bad idea." He frowned and set the phone down. "You realize, we're gonna have one shot at this guy. Once we're blown, it's over. And Nash is going to have our asses either way."

A smile spread across my face.

"But remember, if you're planning to get video from on board that boat, you can't stowaway. For it to be admissible in court, you have to be invited aboard."

I nodded. "Invited. Right." How the hell was I going to do that?

I shot up from the bench, headed for the sink, and went to work washing the dishes. I needed something to do with my hands while I organized my thoughts into some semblance of a plan. Dalton could do them twice later.

I scrubbed and scrubbed, my mind in overdrive. Perhaps they needed another hand on board. Not likely though, as they were already heading out. Maybe pose as a second captain? Probably all set there too. The cook? Maybe we could persuade that Dylan boy to quit. Put flour in his stew?

I stacked the dishes and paced while Dalton got dressed. There had to be a way to get on that boat. Something that man needed. What little I knew of him, which was from our one, short encounter, and as much as I hate to admit Dalton was right about him, he seemed like the kind of man who would be suspicious of my grandma. And if he suspected the agency was on to him at all, there was no way he'd let a stranger on board.

But the son, Michael, might. Yes. He was my ticket. He was my best chance. If I could get his attention, then get him talking, I could figure out what Ray needed. Then I would persuade Michael into thinking I was a valuable asset and get him to convince Ray to invite me aboard.

I slipped into the head and rummaged through my toiletry

bag. A little mascara, some eyeshadow. I swiped some lipstick on my lips.

Dalton was standing in the galley with his arms crossed when I got out.

"How do I look?" I asked.

"Is that lipstick?"

"There's a storm. Where do sailors hang out during a storm? The pub, of course."

"And what are you planning to do?"

"Well, Michael and I had a conversation going and—"

"The son? Are you telling me your plan is to—"

"The oldest trick in the book," I said with a grin.

CHAPTER 9

I fled up the ladder and down the dock before Dalton could say anything more.

The crew of the *Forseti* was at the same table they'd been at two nights before, each with a basket of fish and chips.

I found two empty stools at the bar, leaned on my elbows between them, and ordered a beer. After a moment, I spun around and looked right at Michael and smiled. He noticed. *Good. Now to reel him in.*

The bartender nudged me with my mug of beer. I tipped it back and chugged down a few gulps, then wiped my mouth with the back of my hand, my eyes on Michael.

He said something to the other two of his crew, then rose and walked toward me.

"You're back," he said.

"So are you," I said, letting my eyes travel down to his waist, then back up.

His eyes on my beer, he said, "Kinda early to start, isn't it?"

I shrugged, tilted my head down a little and looked up at him with my best glamour eyes. "What else is there to do?"

He grinned. "Well, you've got me there."

"So you'll join me?"

"Can't think of anything I'd like better."

I waved to the bartender and motioned for him to bring

another beer.

"So, tell me, what's a lady like you doing in a place like this?" Michael said.

"That's a terrible line," I said with a giggle. "Really."

"Yeah, well," he said, all matter-of-fact. "You're not here to fish." He tipped up his beer and looked at me over the bottle.

"True." I took another swig of my beer, stalling. If I was going to get anywhere with this guy, I had to ditch the married couple act. Make it known I was available. But not too easy. "My boyfriend thought it would be great fun to go sailing on vacation." I added a big eye roll.

He raised one eyebrow.

"My *ex* boyfriend, I mean," I added with emphasis. "He turned out to be a real jerk."

He nodded and sipped his beer, taking some time to formulate a response, it seemed. "Are you afraid of him?" he finally said, genuinely concerned.

I hesitated, trying to give him the impression I was, but wouldn't say. It could only help my cause, right? This guy might have been Ray's son, but he didn't seem so bad. Maybe his mom was a good person, one of those Ivy-bred women who took off with a rogue badass like Ray Goldman to piss off her parents. Maybe she'd raised him right, with good manners and a respect for women. He seemed to have a bit of chivalry in him. I could work it. "I've a mind to catch the next ferry out of here," I said. "But I'm stuck. This storm is quite something, isn't it?"

"Yeah, something." His eyes never left mine. He had that intensity of a guy who knows exactly what he wants and doesn't let up until he gets it. And right now, he was focused. On me. *Excellent.*

"I don't know about you," I said, "But I'm feeling a little restless, holed up like this, for days on end."

That broke the spell. He looked away, sipped his beer. "My dad says the storm's clearing already. We're heading back out in the morning."

"Oh?" I said. *Crap.* "Are you sure it will be safe to head out?"

He shrugged, as though he hadn't given it any thought. Either because his father had decided and that was that or he was too manly to let a storm keep him in port. I wasn't sure which.

I hadn't seen any report that the storm was letting up. Was Ray desperate enough to head out in this weather? To take that kind of risk to find the whales? Either way, this was my only chance then. I turned to Michael and gave him my best sexy eyes. "Meanwhile, what's there to do around here that's fun?"

One eyebrow went up. "What about your boyfriend?"

"My *ex* boyfriend."

"Oh, that's right," he said, his eyes all flirty now.

"So...any ideas?"

"Actually, yes." He took my hand in his and said, "There's something I want to show you."

He led me past the pool table, down the narrow hallway, and out the back door to a tiny, grass-roofed shed. The door had been left ajar a few inches. The wind whipped down the alley between the pub and the shed. I hesitated. Why in the world would Michael take me back here? My pulse picked up a bit. Was this a trap?

"Um, I'm sorry if I gave you the impression that I'm that kind of girl." If he expected me to knock one out in the back shed, I'd kick him in the nuts and come up with another plan.

"My, you have an imagination," he said with a warm, disarming smile. "C'mon." He pushed the door open, and with the grin of a boy showing off his older brother's secret clubhouse, he motioned for me to follow him in.

You're being paranoid now. Go with it. I took one step inside behind him and—was that...the mewing of kittens?

A bare light bulb hung over a crate, inside which a heap of little fur balls, maybe four weeks old, snuggled. Someone had rigged the light bulb for warmth. Their little blue eyes were open and they were squirming and crawling over each other. One rolled over, showing its little pot-belly. A gray tabby.

Michael had a conspiratorial grin. "Aren't they cute?"

I picked up the roly-poly one and cuddled it to my cheek. "Oh my, are they ever."

He picked one up and held it to his chest, petting it softly. "You're going to be just fine, little one," he said, then added, "The bartender has been trying to find good homes for them."

I picked up a second one. "Too bad people aren't responsible enough to get their pets spayed and neutered. It really makes me—" I stopped short "—want to take them all." *Crap.* I had to be careful.

"I wish." He grinned and nodded, showing no reaction to my semi-rant.

"You could take one on the boat," I said. "People do it all the time." I set the first one down and picked up another. "Just think, an unlimited supply of fish. A kitty-cat's dream."

He shook his head, but didn't say anything more. He leaned against the wall, stroking the kitten, making little soothing noises.

I leaned on the wall next to him. "They're so sweet," I said, but Michael seemed lost in the simple joy of petting the kitten. I tried to sort out in my mind how he could be on the hunt for an orca, that he could be here in Norway for the sole purpose of capturing one from the wild, yanking it from its ocean home, kidnapping it from its family, yet here he was, all sentimental, cooing at a tiny kitten. How could that be? Certainly it wouldn't be fair to judge someone by his father's behavior. But he was an adult, and there was no way he didn't know what his father was up to. He couldn't possibly be ignorant of the whole plan. But how could the same man do both?

"You surprise me," I said. "I wouldn't have thought you were an animal lover."

"Yeah?" he said. A question.

"You know, being a fisherman and all."

He shrugged, as though one didn't have anything to do with the other. Did he think of the whales as just big fish? Did he have no understanding of them at all? Their intelligence, their capacity to feel, to hurt, to love?

The little kitten purred as he scratched behind its ears.

Maybe he really thought there was nothing wrong with it. Maybe he thought whales were like cats and dogs, easily domesticated. Or maybe he was one of those who think all animals are better off being cared for by humans. Maybe he actually believed what he was doing was a good thing. Back in the 80s, his father had made the claim that what he did was for the greater good, that his work was changing public perception of the killer whale, that they were not to be feared, but admired. He'd claimed that showing them to the world in their special amphitheater-style aquariums did more to further the interest of killer whales than any scientist ever could.

I admit, times were different then. Some of his claims might even have been true. My grandma had taken me to an aquarium when I was a child and no doubt that experience contributed to my life-long love for animals. But that doesn't justify putting the whales through that hell. Not then and not now.

Sure, an argument could be made that back then, Ray, like everyone else, didn't know any better, but the difference was, he'd made a fortune in the process. And now, all these years later, there was no excuse. Pure greed brought him out of retirement—greed for that one-million-dollar price tag.

But what was it for Michael?

Maybe his father had some hold over him, some deep-seated psychological pull. What do they call it? The father complex? Always seeking his father's approval? Had his dad done a number on his confidence? I suppose I was lucky. My dad had always told me I could do anything I wanted, I could accomplish anything I set my mind to. But what had Ray told Michael? To shut up and follow orders? What a different experience of life.

Was that why he was here with him, following like a faithful servant, instead of somewhere living his own life, building his own career?

I'd always been a little baffled by my friends from high school who'd bounced around in different sales clerk jobs or fast food places with no apparent direction. Not me. There'd been no question in my mind where I was headed. At eighteen, I'd enrolled in college, got my bachelor's degree in three and a half years, all the while doing every extracurricular activity I could to make my application to Fish & Wildlife shine. I was on a mission. Every detail planned out and scheduled right down to the minute.

I looked at the man standing beside me. He didn't seem like the kind of guy who'd blindly follow in his father's footsteps. He had a confidence about him that didn't fit that persona. And I couldn't believe he really wanted to be a whale hunter, either. He had a gentle side, a chivalrous side.

Unless this was all an act to get me to sleep with him.

It didn't matter. Maybe I'd never be sure. Right now, I needed him to get me on that boat.

I looked into his eyes. "You're sweet, you know that?"

He put the kitten back in the box. "Another drink?"

"Yeah, sure," I said, handing him one of my kittens and setting the other one down with its mewling fur-ball siblings.

He held the kitten I'd given him, cuddling it to his neck. Then, as he pulled away, he said to me, "You're beautiful, you know that."

"I…" My cheeks flushed pink. "Thank you."

He leaned forward and I leaned forward. And we kissed.

Maybe I'm just a sucker for a man with a kitten, but—wow—was that a kiss. I staggered backward, my insides all squishy.

His eyes held mine and—dammit—I wanted him to kiss me again. *Crap*. I needed to be extra careful with this one.

"Shall we?" he said.

My mouth parted ever so slightly. "Shall we…?"

"Get another drink?"

"Um, yeah, sure," I said.

He set down the kitten, took me by the hand, and led me back into the crowded pub. We took our stools back at the bar and he ordered a couple of drinks. Then he turned to me and said, "The night is still young. What shall we do now?"

I blushed. "Well, I thought maybe—"

The front door swung open and Michael's head swiveled toward the man who walked in. It was Ray, lumbering in like he owned the place. Ray saw Michael right away and scowled.

Michael tensed up, as if fighting an impulse, battling some decision. He seemed more annoyed than intimidated. He chugged down his beer and set the empty bottle on the bar. "I'll catch you later."

Ray certainly had something over him. "I'll be here," I muttered, feeling like a fool. I had been so sure I'd had him on the hook.

Michael sauntered over to the table and eased into a chair with his father and the crew. Ray signaled to the bartender and moments later a round of drinks arrived. Ray held up his mug. "Boys, let's catch us a big fish!"

I wanted to march over there and shove the glass mug down his throat, but I quickly put a smile on my face when I caught Michael looking at me. Then Ray said something to him and he was drawn away.

That boy's got a short leash. This was going to be harder than I thought.

I tried to act bored, like I had all the time in the world. But the clock was ticking.

I sipped my beer.

The men chuckled, slapped each other on the back, the usual men-in-a-pub stuff.

Maybe I needed a different tactic to get Michael's attention back. The man on the bar stool next to me wasn't too old, wasn't too bad looking. In the dark pub. And in desperate times. I turned to him. "What brings you in?"

He looked at me like I'd gone mad, his bushy eyebrows crinkled together into one. "Beer."

"I mean, you know, how was your day?"

The unibrow shot up. "Why? Are you a prostitute?"

My jaw dropped open. *That conversation's not going anywhere.*

Behind me, someone rubbed against my back as he eased onto the bar stool. I swung around. It was Dalton.

"How's it going?" he whispered into my ear.

"Actually, it was going well until Ray arrived. That man is a—"

"Careful," Dalton warned.

"I'm glad you're here. I was just resorting to the make-him-jealous-by-flirting-with-someone-else tactic and, well—" I nodded toward the grump next to me "—this guy wasn't cutting it." I put my hand on Dalton's chest and giggled, a flirtatious gesture. "But you, my dear, might bring him running."

Dalton curled up his lip. "Women and their games." He glanced around the bar. "I'm not so sure this is a good idea."

"Of course it is. What else have we got?"

"I mean, I'm not sure it's worth it. C'mon back to the boat. We'll figure out something else."

"Let's just see how this plays out. I've got a good shot here. I think he's got a chivalrous side. I told him you were my ex-boyfriend, that you'd turned out to be a jerk." I gave him a confident nod and leaned in and whispered, "He took me out back to see some abandoned kittens. You should have seen him."

"Kittens? Really?" He leaned back with an eye roll. "I knew a guy once who borrowed puppies from the pound and walked them in the park to attract single women. He said they were chick magnets."

"Exactly. He's—"

"He's heading back out on a fishing boat for weeks. Trust me. He's just trying to get in your pants."

I shrugged. "Exactly."

"Don't tell me," Dalton said, going on as if he hadn't heard a word I'd said. "He told you you're beautiful."

"What is wrong with—" I drew in a breath. "You're jealous."

"Jealous? Pff." He shook his head. "Be serious."

"I'm dead serious. You don't like that he's really into me."

"What I don't like is this whole approach. You're not thinking of the full picture here. Of course he's into you. Maybe you're blinded a little by this guy's attention."

I sat back. "I beg your pardon."

"This guy could be—" He paused, realizing he'd been raising his voice. He glanced around, then leaned in close. "If you go down this road—"

"I can handle it." I was getting irritated now. Why couldn't Dalton support me? I knew this would work. "Just go with it."

Dalton shook his head. "I've got a bad feeling about this. Something's not right." He patted me on the arm and rose to go. "C'mon, let's just go."

"No. You go if you want. I'm not giving up on this," I said in a loud whisper. "You need to trust me for once."

"Is there a problem here?"

Our heads snapped to the speaker. Michael stood there, his hands on his hips.

I glared at Dalton. *Ha! Told you it would work.*

Dalton looked from Michael to me, then back to Michael. A shadow passed over his eyes. A surrender. A decision. "No problem," he said to Michael and put his arm around me, pulling me snug up against him.

"I'd like to hear it from the lady," Michael said.

"Well, I—"

"Buzz off," Dalton said. "Mind your own business."

Michael didn't budge. "I'm making this my business. Now get your hands off the lady."

Dalton huffed and turned on the bar stool to face Michael. "What's your problem?"

Michael looked at me, then back to Dalton and I swear he thrust his chest forward. "You're my problem."

"Oh yeah?" said Dalton. He swung high and punched Michael square in the jaw.

CHAPTER 10

Michael staggered backward, his eyes wide. Then, in a flash, his expression changed to rage. He charged forward, fists in front of him, jabbing at Dalton.

Dalton swung wide, missing Michael's jaw.

Michael grabbed hold of Dalton's shirt and pulled him from the stool and slammed him into a table. Dalton caught his balance and managed to stay on his feet.

Michael stepped back and shoved up his sleeves. Dalton lunged at him, all bluff and no force. This wasn't the Dalton I knew. He was faking. But why? Why had he thrown that punch to begin with? *What the hell is going on?*

The other men in the bar were on their feet, roaring amid the ruckus, shouting, "Hit 'em again! Knock 'em down!"

Michael managed to land a punch, then another, in the jaw, then in the stomach. He was beating the crap out of him. Dalton doubled over but didn't fight back.

I stepped between them. "Stop! Stop it!"

Dalton snarled at me, his lip puffy and bleeding. "Stay out of it."

"That's no way to treat a lady," Michael spat and slammed Dalton with a right hook. Dalton fell back into the table.

"Knock it off, boys!" hollered the bartender.

Michael ignored him and grabbed Dalton by the collar, dragging him to his feet. Dalton yanked free and head-butted him in the stomach and the two slammed to the floor.

The men in the bar roared.

They rolled, one on top of the other, fists flying. Michael got up on one knee, then to his feet and landed a kick in Dalton's side.

Why wasn't Ray breaking it up? I glanced around the bar, but he was nowhere to be seen. Maybe Michael had waited for Ray to leave and that's when he saw Dalton with me?

I grabbed Michael by the arm. "Stop! Please stop!" I wanted to beat him to a bloody pulp myself, right then and there. Michael stepped back, huffing, his eyes on Dalton.

Dalton got to his feet, grabbed me by the wrist, spun me around, and planted a big kiss on my lips. "Now step back, sweetheart." In his eyes I could see he meant it.

He went after Michael again, arms flailing with no measured target. It must have been hard for Dalton, a Navy SEAL, to pull his punches and take the fall. Why it was necessary was beyond me. What the hell was this going to prove? *Men!*

Michael on the other hand wasn't holding back. He'd obviously been in a few bar brawls in his time and he was a heavyweight. He went after Dalton with a hook, then a jab to the kidney. Dalton doubled over and Michael caught him in the jaw.

The bartender had finally had enough. He shouted to a couple of the regulars, "Get 'em outta here."

"Let 'em fight it out," one said.

Dalton hadn't had enough. He charged Michael again and they slammed into another table.

Bjørn, the old man on the boat, the helmsman Michael had said, grabbed Michael by the arm. "That's enough, now. A broken arm won't do on a fishing boat." He gave him a stern look. "You've made your point. Now leave him be."

Michael shoved the man away.

Someone grabbed hold of my arm. I spun around. It was the bartender. "You're leaving," he said.

"What?"

"You're the cause of it." He dragged me toward the door. "Now get out and don't come back."

I looked back toward Dalton. A hefty man, a six-foot-something-mountain-of-muscle was hauling him to his feet.

"You, too," the bartender told him, waving his wet rag at him. "Out!"

Dalton stumbled out the front door after me, holding his side.

Right behind him was Michael, Bjørn ushering him along. Michael brushed Bjørn off. "Hey, babe," he said when he saw me. "You all right?"

I nodded.

Bjørn whispered something in his ear and urged him toward the docks. Michael nodded to Bjørn and went with him.

I stood there like a dope, watching him go, not knowing what to do. Follow? Tell him thanks for saving me? Then what? I had no reference for dealing with this neanderthal behavior. If he'd have been a real-life date, I'd have already been out of there without looking back.

Dalton was limping toward our boat. I caught up to him. "What the hell was all that for?" I asked him. "You couldn't let it go. Now you've ruined my only chance to get on that boat. What the hell is your problem? Why can't you trust me?"

He shook his head and didn't answer.

"Men!" I planted my feet and watched him hobble toward the *Sea Mist*.

I spun on my heel and marched to the same bench and called back my friend Chris.

He answered right away. "Dr. Chris."

"Very funny."

"What's happened now?"

"What? I don't just call when I have problems."

Silence.

"Okay. You're not going to believe this." As I paced in front of the bench, I told him about my plan, how, for some reason, Dalton didn't like it and wouldn't support me. "And now this. He goes and picks a fight with the guy. In a bar. Ruining my only chance for a shot at him. I mean, what the hell?"

"Well, Poppy, I'm not sure—"

"What's his problem anyway? I bet he's pissed because I came up with an idea, a brilliant idea I might add, and he didn't think of it. Men, I swear. He couldn't stand having to play second fiddle, on the sidelines, backing me up for once."

"Poppy, maybe he's—"

"This guy's got it in for me. He doesn't want me for a partner, so this is his way of getting rid of me. Making me look bad. Sure, he wants to act like Mr. Nice Guy, all apologetic about Costa Rica, then this. You should have seen him, Chris. I had that guy eating out of the palm of my hand. He was frothing at the mouth. He was going to tell me everything I wanted to know and then some." I took a breath. "Dammit!" I plopped down on the bench.

"Are you done yet?"

"No!" I got back up.

Silence.

"You know what, I'm going to march over there and tell him what a jerk he is."

"Poppy?"

"What!"

"Did you call me to rant all night or for my advice? Because I've got a long flight in the morning and—"

"Your advice."

He waited.

"Okay, to rant, and I thank you, my very best friend, master listener, knower-of-all-the-right-things-to-say." I huffed. "All right, go ahead with the advice."

"Ask *him* why he did it."

"That's your advice? He's not going to tell me—"

"Poppy. Ask him."

I slumped down on the bench. "Fine."

When I got back to the boat, I found he had managed to get down the ladder on his own. I got some ice and held it to his cheek. His left eye was swollen shut, his cheek bloody.

"What were you thinking? Why in the world did you throw that first punch? I had him. Dammit, Dalton. I had him. I had him on the hook."

He took hold of the bag of ice and winced as he held it to his eye. "You wanted to do it your way."

"What?" He must have gotten his brain scrambled in the melee.

He looked at me with innocent eyes. "So we did it your way."

"What the hell are you talking about?" He did get his brain scrambled.

"Seriously?" He grinned and started to snicker, then held his stomach. "Where'd you grow up, anyway?"

I sat back and looked at him. "Why does that sound like an insult?"

"Guys like that—" He wiped blood from his lip and looked at it on his finger. "It's all about conquering, about possession. You were dangling the hook. I set it."

I stared at him. What could I say?

"Don't you watch National Geographic? Those big horn rams bucking their heads together. Polar bears wrestling. Even the whales ram each other for a female. The narrator always says they are fighting to continue their bloodline." He smirked. "They just want to get laid."

I clamped my teeth together. "So you…this whole thing was…all about testosterone?"

"Listen to me. You be careful. You're playing with fire."

I turned away from him. He was right. But I could handle it.

I opened the equipment locker, found the first aid kit, and sorted through the bandages and ointment. "Look at you," I said. "You're bleeding and you're—"

"I'm fine. I got it," Dalton said, waving me off. "What are you still doing here? You going to let me get the crap beat out of me for nothing? You wanted on that boat. Now go get on it."

I stared at him. "And you'll tell Nash…?"

He grinned. "Well, probably wouldn't sound so good if I told him you'd been kicked out of two bars already."

I started up the ladder, but stopped and climbed back down. Sure, I might be able to reel Michael in, get him to talk, but would he really get me on the boat with him? My luck, he really did just expect a sleazy romp in the lifeboat with the plan to disappear in the night. I needed an edge. I needed a slam dunk.

"Toss me the phone."

"Sure," said Dalton. "What are you thinking?"

"Michael said they're leaving in the morning. I've got one shot at this." I punched in Dr. Parker's number. "I need some advice."

Finally, on the seventh ring she picked up.

"Uh, hi, this is Poppy. Listen, I need to know as much as you can tell me about these fishing boats, how it works, what I could do that would be irresistibly useful."

"How would that help?"

"I'm trying to get on the boat."

"But they aren't actually fishing, right?"

"Well, right, but I need to have a reason to be invited on board, something that I know about fishing that would be useful capturing an orca. Maybe something they haven't thought of or I don't know." I turned so Dalton couldn't hear me. "I know it's a long shot, but…"

"What kind of boat is he on?"

"An old fishing trawler. Purse seine nets, I think."

"That's hard work. He'd never hire you. He wouldn't believe you could do it. You can cook, right?"

"Yeah, but he has a cook."

"Can't you put something in his stew? Get him fired or something."

"It had crossed my mind," I said with a chuckle. She and I were kindred spirits. "But they're heading out to sea in the morning. I've been working an angle, batting my eyelashes. Got a crewman's attention, the son actually, but I need something more."

"Okay, okay. I'm thinking." I could hear her tapping a pencil on something. "Is the boat big enough for an on-board tank? One large enough to keep the orca submersed?"

"No. That's the thing. It's a really small boat."

She was thinking. "So he plans to use a drag net for transport?"

"The thing is, Dr. Parker, I have no idea. I suppose he could use a drag net. I didn't realize that was an option." I looked at Dalton and shrugged. He shrugged. He hadn't been aware of that technique either. "Unless he'd put the whales right on deck."

"God, I hope not. They'd never survive it." She was quiet for some time. "This doesn't make sense. I can't imagine he has a holding facility nearby in Norway. I figured he planned to transport on board. This guy must be a complete amateur."

"He's no amateur. He's been doing this since the 60s."

"Maybe that's the biggest boat he could afford? Or he's planning to meet up with another boat?"

"The transport boat?" I said.

"Maybe, but that would mean extra work. Extra stress on the animals," she said with a sigh. "Well, whatever he's planning, at some point he'll be yanking one from the water. Their bodies aren't designed for it. Even if he has a proper harness, if he gets one on board, he'll have to keep its body temperature down with sea water, or even ice. Did you see anything on board for that?"

"I didn't get a good look—"

"This is tragic," she huffed, exasperated. "He's just going to kill them. No matter how he plans to transport, the odds of survival are slim. The risk is so high." She paused. "At least back in the days when it was legal to capture they usually had a veterinarian on board who knew about the—"

"A veterinarian?"

"I don't know how any reputable—"

My feet were already in motion. I handed Dalton the phone. "Get all the info you can on how to care for a killer whale during transport. I'll be back."

He raised his eyebrows. "You want me to—" he gestured toward the phone.

"What? You're tired of flirting?" I shoved the phone at him.

CHAPTER 11

I went straight back to the pub and flung the front door open. No one much cared that I was there save for the bartender. He threw down his wet towel and lumbered over to me. "I told you not to come back."

Michael wasn't anywhere I could see, so I frowned at the grumpy old man and backed out of the door. I'd learned what I wanted to know. Ray was back, and Dylan and Bjørn were there. That meant Michael was likely back on the *Forseti*. Alone.

I raced down the docks to the boat. Should I just step aboard? Etiquette says no. But how else would I get to him?

I crossed the deck and banged on the door to the galley. I could see there was no one inside, but if he was down below, he should hear me. After what seemed like forever, I went up the stairs to the wheelhouse and peeked in the window. He wasn't in there either. *Now what?*

Where else would he be? I went back toward the pub and slumped down on my now favorite street bench. The wind howled down the street. A plastic bag whipped in circles at the corner of the building. I held onto my hair with one hand to keep it out of my face and watched a raven hippety-hoppin' on the sidewalk, plucking at some tidbit of a snack floating in a giant mud puddle.

"Yer lookin' for Michael, ain't yer."

I looked up. It was Dylan, the gangly young man, the one Michael had said was the cook and deckhand.

"You know where he is?" I asked.

He had the expression of a child expecting to be punished for spilling his milk. He looked down at his hands, fiddled with his fingers. "If yer don't mind me askin', why's a bonny lady loike yer loike 'im anyway. It don't make naw sense."

I shrugged. "You're right. Sometimes the heart doesn't make any sense."

"Ain't dat de truth," he said and plopped down next to me, then unfurled his long legs out in front of him.

He seemed like a genuine, kind soul. Made me wonder if he had the slightest inkling what Ray was really up to. And what he would do when he found out. He might make a good ally, but I couldn't risk testing those waters now.

"So do you know where I can find him?"

He examined his boot laces, then scratched behind his ear. He pointed down the road. "Proobably de church," he said. "Sometimes yer man goes dare."

"Is he a religious man?" That'd be good to know.

"Oi don't tink so." He scrunched up his face in thought. "Proobably figures it's de last place 'is auld paddy wud luk."

I nodded. "Thanks. Dylan, right?"

His eyes brightened. "Yeah, Dylan."

An old stave church, one of the few remaining that had been completely constructed of wood during the Middle Ages, stood at the end of the road, its shingled steeple pointing upward, toward the heavens.

As I approached, I admired the intricately-carved timbers that criss-crossed over the entry. The large wooden door was adorned with swirling etchings that looked like angel's wings and reindeer with ornately-curved antlers.

If I hadn't been here for work, I could've spent hours learning the history of this place. The architecture alone was fascinating. I was tempted to take a quick walk around the outside, check it out, but I didn't want to risk missing Michael.

The iron hinges creaked as I pushed the heavy wooden door open and stepped inside.

A gust of wind followed me in, past the rows of pews, all the way to the altar, where a single candle burned below a simple wooden cross. The flame flickered and danced before it settled again to a peaceful glow, long after the door had closed behind me and my eyes had adjusted to the dim light inside.

As far as I could tell, I had the place to myself. Michael was nowhere in sight.

I silently stepped from the entry area into the empty sanctuary, my eyes drawn to the vaulted ceiling, suspended by ancient wooden timbers, and the painted cherubs and fluffy clouds that seemed to hover between earth and the celestial realm. The scent of incense lingered in the air. The place had a peaceful, dreamlike quality. Timeless. I could picture the Vikings, crowded into the long pews, horned helmets in their laps, tamed by the angelic choir and the gentle words of the priest. I almost envied the serenity they must have felt here, in this place of respite from their lives of constant conflict.

I sat down in the fourth pew from the back. Now what? Was I to pray to find Michael?

I wasn't much for church or religion. Nature was my sanctuary, the natural order, my code. But I had to admit, the solace some found in "giving it all up to God" was appealing. Comforting even. For those who believed. And this building made me feel it.

I don't claim to have any answers. I suppose that makes me agnostic. I just don't know. Maybe there is some invisible, guiding force in the universe. The sense of awe when I entered this old church was enough to give me pause, cause me to reflect, recognize that I was but a tiny speck in a vast universe, that my tiny, insignificant problems were just that—insignificant.

The only thing that truly mattered was love and goodness and living a good life. Wasn't that the point of religion?

What baffles me most is how, for so many, the call to be compassionate, caring, doesn't extend to animals. I know there is a debate over the very words of the Bible, as written in the book of Genesis, as to whether God intended the animals of the world to be here for the use of humankind or that humankind was to be the steward of all the animals and the environment. For me, the answer is clear. We are part of the animal world as sure as we live and breathe. Only arrogance keeps humans separate from it, that assumption that somehow humans alone have an elite birthright.

Interesting, how here, in this church, the walls are adorned with magnificent murals that prominently portray the animals of this region, obviously with great reverence. The antler motif repeats throughout. When did we give up this respect for the other living creatures among us? Seems it somehow coincided with our gaze being drawn ever skyward.

A door to the side of the altar squeaked open and the Reverend appeared.

Suddenly I realized that I didn't know what denomination this church was. Catholic, probably, right? Anglican? One of those that had taken over during the Protestant Reformation? I glanced around. No obvious confessionals. Is that what Michael had been doing? Confessing? Was he feeling guilt over his quest to capture a whale? Or was it the fight with Dalton that concerned him?

The Reverend approached me, his arms hanging comfortably in front of him, one hand holding the other. He wore street clothes, but I could tell by his manner, he was the reverend. And the kind smile, rosy cheeks. In fact, he looked a lot like Reverend Alden from *Little House on the Prairie,* the only Reverend I've ever known.

"May I help you, young lady?"

I shook my head. "No, thank you. I'm actually just here

looking for a friend."

"Ah," he said with a knowing nod. He glanced toward the door from whence he had come, then patted me on the shoulder. "Perhaps you need only to be patient."

I pointed to the door. "So he's…?"

A warm smile lit up his face. His eyes even seemed to sparkle. He nodded again, reassuring me, but gave no explanation. "I've someone to visit," he said. "But stay as long as you'd like." I watched him walk down the aisle and stop briefly in the vestibule for his raincoat, then push through the heavy door.

I turned around and leaned back in the pew. Patience, huh?

About thirty seconds later, Michael shuffled through the door. To look at him now, I could barely tell he'd been in a fight, save for the cut on his cheek and red knuckles. Dalton had taken most of the hits.

Michael saw me, but his expression didn't change. He ambled down the aisle and eased into the pew next to me.

"What's a lady like you doing in a place like this?" he whispered.

I couldn't resist a tiny smirk. *Adorable.* "I got kicked out of the pub and didn't want to go back to the boat so I—" I fiddled with the hymnal. Why play coy? "I was looking for you, actually."

He turned to me and smiled like a hyena on the prowl. "Yeah? How'd you know where to find me?"

"A little Irish bird."

He grinned and nodded.

"I wouldn't have guessed you were a religious man." Or a cat lover, actually.

"I'm not," he said with a slight shake of his head. "I just like it here, you know. The solitude. I can think."

I glanced around the sanctuary. "I know what you mean." My eyes found his again. "It keeps me humble."

He let go a laugh.

"I get it though, living on a boat. Close quarters and all."

I blew out my breath. "Especially with someone you don't like."

He smirked. "My dad can be trying."

"I lived on a boat with my dad for an entire summer when I was a kid." *Why'd I just share that?*

"Really?" He turned to face me.

"A sailboat." I started to chew my thumbnail, then yanked it back out of my mouth. "My dad died right after that."

His eyes turned soft. "I'm sorry."

"Yeah, well, it was…" I shrugged.

He turned back toward the altar. "Life's funny sometimes, isn't it? Here you are, back on a sailboat. What do you suppose that means?"

"That I'm crazy?"

"I was thinking it might mean"—his eyebrow shot up— "you've got a thing for sailors."

My turn to smirk. "Maybe you're right." I looked away. "My dad was the captain of my world. I swore one day I'd marry a man like him." Why was I being so honest with this guy?

"Is that why you agreed to go sailing with"—he jerked his thumb toward the marina—"*him*? You thought you'd marry him some day?"

"I could ask you the same question. Why are you on a boat with your dad, thousands of miles from home, when it sounds like you two don't get along."

He looked at me for a long time, his stare laced with suspicion. Or maybe he was contemplating an answer. Finally, he said, "You don't want to talk about him. I get it. So you turn the tables."

"Or maybe that's what you're doing right now?" I held his gaze. "It's okay. I didn't mean to pry. Your relationship with your father is your business."

"There's nothing to tell." He flashed me a disarming grin. "A man's gotta make a living, right?"

We both turned back toward the altar and sat in silence for a while. When he started to fidget, I whispered, "I'm sorry about my boyfriend."

His one eyebrow shot upward. "I thought he was your *ex* boyfriend."

"Yeah," I said. "Definitely."

I smiled. He smiled.

The wind whistled through the rafters and the timbers creaked.

I placed my hand on his. "I suppose I shouldn't have followed you here. It's just that, I know you're leaving in the morning and I didn't want you to go without saying goodbye."

"Where will you go now?" he asked. "And don't tell me you're staying with *him*."

"I don't know. I don't really have anywhere to go." I turned away, drew in a breath like I was fighting back tears. "I don't even know where I'm sleeping tonight." *Okay, here goes nothing.* I turned back and let my gaze linger on his lips. "I thought maybe…"

His breathing changed, more shallow. His eyes lowered to my breasts.

I turned away. "I'm sorry. You must think I'm a…" I covered my eyes with my hands. "I'm just, I don't know, frustrated." I turned back, tears in my eyes. "I had dreams, you know. When I got out of college, I thought I'd have a position right away. Maybe even open my own practice." I lowered my head and fiddled with my thumbnail. "I was so naive."

He shifted in the seat. "You went to college? What for?"

Atta boy. "Veterinary school." A hint of interest flashed in his eyes. Good. "I love horses, you know. But the business. You gotta know somebody." I shrugged. "The only internship I could get was at the Detroit Zoo." I hesitated. I had to be careful not to lay it on too thick. Thankfully, my verbal blunder about spaying and neutering the kittens could turn to my favor. "For three months I took care of the hedgehogs. Can you believe it? *Hedgehogs.*" I raised my eyebrows. "Do you know how to take the body temperature of a hedgehog?"

He shook his head. "Not sure I want to know." Something in his demeanor had changed. Subtle. He hid it well. But I could see he was thinking, pondering. Was he trying to figure out how to get me to come with him now without seeming too forward?

"Trust me. You don't." I sighed, let my shoulders slump. "I'll be lucky if I can get a job in some big city neutering feral cats."

Michael didn't say anything in response. His eyes fixed on his hands in his lap and I wasn't sure where to take the conversation from here. If I drove it home, I risked being too obvious.

I sat silently next to him for a while.

Finally, he said, "Well, we still have tonight."

Crap. He was either testing me or I'd misjudged him. I was going to have to take it up a notch. "I'm sorry. I was mistaken." I rose to leave.

He took hold of my hand. "What do you mean?"

I spun on him. "I thought you were my knight in shining armor. But I see now, you're just like all the rest." I pursed my lips. "I need to get out of here. Do something exciting." I looked him in the eyes. "Something bold. Like the Vikings, you know." I let my eyes travel to the ceiling, around the sanctuary, like I was being inspired. "Sail into the sunset, destined for new horizons. Conquer the world." *Geez. I should audition for a soap opera.* "You know what I mean?"

"Yeah, sure, I guess," he said.

Now we were in a careful cat and mouse game. I had one chance at this. *Here goes…* I plopped down and leaned back in the pew. "Maybe I'll just stowaway on your boat," I muttered. "Now that'd be a story to tell my kids someday."

He took my hand in his and said, "Maybe we could work something out. You know, just so you don't have to go back to him."

I laid my head on his shoulder. "You're kind. But don't worry. I can take care of myself. Besides, I'm sure your father would never—"

"You let me worry about my father."

I tilted my head back and he gave me a passionate kiss.

This better be worth it.

CHAPTER 12

As we walked down the dirt road, the wind still whipping in my hair, I snuggled against him, stroking his ego, when doubt creeped back unbidden. Maybe he wasn't what he seemed. Could it be that he and his father were already suspicious? And they were setting a trap for me? Get me on board, then once we were out to sea they'd—I shook the thought from my mind. If I was going to go for it, I was going for it. If something happened once I was on board, I'd deal with it when it happened. I could take care of myself.

When we got to the docks, the sun had already set, even though it was late afternoon. This close to the Arctic Circle the days were getting shorter fast. The sun seemed in a hurry to hide for good. The snow and cold, I could take. But nearly twenty-four hours of darkness. How do they do it?

Ray was in the wheelhouse when Michael brought me on board. Michael gestured for me to wait on deck. "Give me a minute," he muttered, his eyes on the wheelhouse as though it were a castle turret guarded by a fire-breathing dragon.

"Sure," I said. *Now we'll see what you're made of. Are you my knight or not?*

He drew in a breath, as if to gather some courage, climbed the stairs to the wheelhouse, and shut the door behind him. He was making a good show of it, anyway.

I could see Ray through the windows, shaking his head, his

frown making his caveman brow even more pronounced. As Michael continued to talk, Ray strutted to and fro. I bet his knuckles were dragging on the floor.

C'mon Michael. You've got all the pieces to the puzzle. You can convince him.

Ray leaned against the window to look out at me. Something in his eyes—the calculating stare of a stalking tiger, as menacing and fixed with threat—made me want to bolt. His pacing suddenly seemed more like that of a predator trapped in a cage.

I smiled wide, all innocent, my feet planted firmly where I stood.

Ray shook his head again.

Finally, Michael slinked from the wheelhouse and I could tell by his body language that it was over. He wouldn't make eye contact with me. I wasn't getting on the boat. Michael had been my best option and he turned out to be a waste of time. I wanted to slap him for being so spineless. I'd misjudged him all along. I thought we'd been playing a delicate dance, a careful maneuvering, a duet of deception.

"So?" I asked.

"My father says no."

Maybe he needed a good-old surge of testosterone. I wrapped my arms around his shoulders and practically stuck my tongue in his ear. "Did you tell him I don't eat much? I swear I'll stay out of the way."

He shook his head as he put his hands on my waist. "It's not that. It's—"

"What? I can work. I need a job anyway. There must be something I could do on board." I smiled, hopeful. "I can cook."

"We got Dylan." He frowned, but his eyes were trained on me, steady, calculating. He was thinking. Or making a show that he was thinking. The wheels were turning. Was he testing me now? "Anything else you can do?"

Was he serious?

"I'm sorry," he said, shaking his head. "Hey, the storm's going to pass. I'm sure the ferry will be running again tomorrow." The edge of his lip slowly curved upward. "I wish you well."

Dammit! "Thanks. Maybe if things were different, huh?"

"Yeah," he said, his eyes revealing nothing.

I scrambled down the ladder on the *Sea Mist*.

Dalton was at the table amid a tangle of power cords.

"Everything charged and ready?" I asked.

"Yep. Double checked each camera." He scribbled in a notebook. "All's ready."

I nodded and slumped onto the seat. "Great."

His eyes refocused on me. "What happened?"

"No go."

"Are you sure?"

"I really worked the vet angle with Michael," I said. "And he played coy about it. I was sure I had him. Then he went to talk to Ray." I ran my finger across my throat.

Dalton nodded, thinking.

"Maybe I could stowaway. Then, once we are out to sea, I get them to agree to let me stay aboard. Technically, that'd do it, right? Then I could plant the camera."

"I"m not sure that—"

"But, I don't know, Michael's too…"

"Too what?"

I let my head flop back, examined the ceiling for inspiration. "He's too clever." I sat back up and looked Dalton in the eye. "But there's got to be a way. I'm telling you. I have him on the hook."

"No doubt. I mean,"—he flashed me that grin of his—"you had me at hello."

I grabbed a pillow and smacked him with it.

Footsteps clomped onto the deck. "'ey! Poppy, ye down dare? 'ey!"

I leapt from my chair and climbed the ladder.

Dylan was in the cockpit. "Dare yer are. I've been lookin' everywhere," he said, out of breath.

"What? Why?"

"'tis Ray. Our Captain. 'e's 'urt."

"What do you mean? What's happened?"

"Dunno," he said with a shrug. "Michael sent me ter git yer."

"Sure, sure. Let's go," I said with a sideways glance to Dalton.

We raced down the dock to the *Forseti*. I followed Dylan up the stairs and into the wheelhouse. Ray lay on his belly on the bench, his face contorted with ornery discomfort.

Michael greeted me. "Thanks for coming."

"What's happened?"

"He had an accident."

Ray had his hand shoved down his pants, clamped onto his left butt cheek.

"What kind of accident?"

"Dylan, thanks. You can go," said Michael. When the door clicked shut, he turned to me. "You said you're a vet. That's a doctor, right?"

"Well, I…" *Crap.* "What kind of injury is it, exactly?"

Ray grimaced.

"Right. Why don't I just take a look." *Yeah, that's it. Show me your bare ass.*

I peeled back his waistband and tugged his pants down, trying to keep a straight face. Ray reluctantly let me pull his hand away. Blood gushed from a gouge down the side of his butt cheek. *Eeeew!* My throat constricted and I turned my head to hide a gag. I grabbed his hand and placed it back over the wound. "Hold it tight," I said, swallowed hard, and turned to Michael. "What happened?"

Ray scowled. "It doesn't matter. Just fix it."

Sure. Right. Was this a test? No way. He wouldn't actually injure himself to see if I was lying, would he? "We need to get you to a hospital. You need stitches."

"No hospital," Ray said.

"Sir, I don't think you're—"

Michael stepped between us, his arms crossed. "You do it."

"Me?" *Crap. Double crap.*

"You're a doctor ain't ya?"

"Well, yes, but"—*Oh. My. God.*—"I don't have any instruments, any supplies." I gestured around the room. "Nothing's sterile. Besides, it's Norway. No worries on the cost. Let's just take him to the hospital."

Michael shook his head. "He stays on the boat." His eyes turned cold. "And you're going to fix him up." It wasn't a request.

"All right. All right," I said, stalling, trying to act like that was a perfectly normal demand. "Well, do you have a first-aid kit on board?"

Michael reached for a box and shoved it at me. "Here."

My mom's the doctor. Not me. This was a serious wound. And, well, I hate blood and guts and bodily fluids. Sure, I had field triage training. But that was ketchup. This was real... *blood.*

Why me? I could get a desk job. Shuffle papers. Yeah, that'd be good. I could be happy.

I set the box down and rummaged through the kit. Ray needed stitches, that was clear. But I probably needed to stop the bleeding to be able to stitch him up. And what about infection? Wait a minute. Did I care if Ray got an infection? I suppose if I was a real doctor and not a quack. Ha, ha. *Oh my god, I'm losing it.*

No, you can do this. Straight face.

One thing about doctors: in a crisis, they take charge. My mom always did. To Michael I said, "Get something to prop up his legs. I want the wound higher than his heart." That's what my mom would say.

Michael didn't question. He just did as I said, grabbing a blanket and pillow from Bjørn's cubby.

"I'm also going to need water to flush the wound. Preferably pressurized. Squirt bottle, hose. Something."

He nodded and pushed through the door.

"You might have a risk of infection," I said to Ray. "Depends on what you were cut with. Do you want to tell me how this happened?"

"Just stitch it up," he grumbled.

Stitches. I had no idea how to do medical stitches. *Bitches!* When I was young, and my mom was going through one of her phases, she tried to teach me how to needlepoint, but I didn't have the patience, nor the desire. All my stitches were misaligned and sloppy. *Rip it out and do it right*, she'd harp. I could hear her voice now, *nice, tight stitches, pay attention. Take pride in your work.* Egads. It was a damn pillow for the cat. I knew he couldn't care less about perfect stitches.

I pushed her out of my head. Triage—that's what this was. Backcountry first-aid. "Good old duct tape will do the trick," I said. "Got any?"

He shook his head. "How do I know?"

Michael came through the door with more pillows and a water bottle. "This do?"

"Yep. Got any duct tape?"

He stopped short. "What?"

"You know, duct tape? Gray, comes on a roll."

"I know what duct tape is. What do you want that for?"

"Well, he needs stitches, and like I said, I don't have the proper supplies. Duct tape is actually a strong, secure option." *Man, I'm blowing some serious smoke.*

"Okay. I'll find some," he said and pushed back out the door again.

I propped Ray's ass up with the pillows, then piled a handful of gauze pads on the wound and had him hold them. I was tempted to snap a quick picture with my cell phone to text to the guys back at Headquarters. They were never going to believe this.

Michael returned with a roll of duct tape in hand.

"Start ripping it off in lengths, about five or six inches. Then I want you to cut them into tiny strips."

"Yes, ma'am," he said.

Yes, *ma'am*? Pshaw!

"Here's what's going to happen. I'm going to wash out the wound, then dry it and contain the bleeding. I want those strips ready so I can get them applied quickly." *If I don't throw up.*

Michael went to work. I put the hand to Ray's forehead, faking like I was taking his temperature. Then everything was ready. I drew in a breath.

Here goes nothing.

I removed the bloodied gauze. Bloody gunk stuck to his ass and oozed. I coughed and a little throw-up lodged in the back of my throat. I squeezed the water bottle, flushing the wound, trying not to actually look at it, then tamped it dry with another gob of clean gauze. I pushed a splurt of triple-biotic ointment onto it, then holding his skin tight with one hand—*oh, for the love of God!*—I placed strips of duct tape crosswise, all along the gash. Then I ripped off a big piece of tape, and laid it down across the strips. "There, that ought to do the trick," I said, my doctor face on. "Keep it clean, try not to rip it open again, and"—I handed the tube of ointment to Michael—"put this on it every day."

His eyes traveled from me to his father's bloody, duct-taped ass cheek. "I don't think so."

"He can do it then," I said, holding back a smirk.

Michael nodded. "That it?"

"Unless you've changed your mind and would like to go to the hospital."

He shook his head. "Thanks."

"No problem." I stood there for a moment, wondering what I could do to convince him to let me go with them. "Okay, then. Take care." I headed for the door.

Michael called after me. "Maybe you should come with us, you know, in case he needs you again."

"You mean, on the boat? Out to sea?"

Ray shook his head as if reluctant. "Yeah, on the boat," he grumbled.

You bet your bloody ass! "Are you sure? I don't want to be in the way and—"

"Go get your bag," Ray said, as though resigned to it. "We leave before daybreak."

Michael winked at me.

"Yes, sir."

Dalton was nodding but he didn't look happy. He was tense, his jaw tight.

"What?" I said. "It's going to work. I told you. Michael likes me."

"I know. That's what I'm afraid of." His voice sounded like he'd just swallowed a dry piece of meat.

"What are you saying?"

"Just that this guy is going to have—" he clenched and unclenched his jaw "—expectations."

"Actually, he's pretty sweet," I said. "Besides, I can handle myself." I was getting irritated and I wasn't sure why. I headed for my bunk to grab my bag.

Dalton followed me. "Like you did with that Noah guy in Costa Rica?"

I spun around to face him. "That was different and you know it."

"Yeah, well, fine, but with this guy, what are you gonna do?"

"What am I gonna do about what?"

He stared at me, stone-faced.

"I'll handle it." *Somehow*.

He was blocking the door. "Yeah, but what if—"

"Dalton!" I shoved him in the stomach. "You're really starting to piss me off."

"All I'm sayin' is you don't have to do this. We're not even supposed to be here. We could head home right now. Get a new assignment."

"What happened to *I got all beat up for you, don't blow it?*"

He blinked one eye. The swollen one. "Something's not right. It was too easy. We should take a step back. There'll be another shot at him. We should go back to Headquarters and—"

"Like hell. I'm not leaving. Not while that man is out capturing killer whales. Not if there's anything I can do about it."

"But these aren't cub scouts we're talking about, Poppy," he said, failing to contain his mounting frustration. "What are you going to do once you're on board anyway? How will you possibly get the video we need without putting your life at risk? Have you really thought this through?"

"Have I thought—" I looked Dalton up and down, my molars clenched together so hard I thought they might crack. He was looking back at me with those eyes. Neither of us moved, stuck in this emotional standoff.

Finally, into the silence, his voice shaky, he said, "You could get hurt. Or worse. You can't just expect me to—" He released the pent up air from his lungs and closed his eyes.

All my anger fluttered out of me like air from a balloon. "You're worried about me."

"Poppy, you are so—" He looked away.

"Admit it. It's because you don't trust me."

He crossed his arms, which made his biceps look huge. "You're a trained agent. Like you said, you can take care of yourself. But you're my partner and partners are supposed to work together, not—" He covered his face with both hands, then ran his fingers through his hair, and looked right at me with exasperation. "Do you have any idea what it's like to be your partner?"

"Well, I…"

His anger was gone. He seemed defeated, exhausted.

"Poppy. You're smart, you're clever, you're…more than capable of handling yourself. But…" He looked away, thinking, then his eyes came back to mine. "My god, you're this red-headed whirlwind. It's like you're on this mission to save the world. By tomorrow. And nothing better get in your way. Nothing and no one. Including me." He shook his head. "It's like you think I'm the enemy here, the one who's blocking your way. You want to do everything on your terms, your way. But there's a reason we have procedures, a reason we plan, and strategize, and, and," he threw his hands up, "and not fly by the seat of our pants. It puts everyone in danger."

Suddenly, the extent of my own myopia astonished me. He was right. I hadn't stopped to think. I hadn't considered for a moment what position I'd put him in, whether he was willing to risk what I was.

"You might be willing to die for these animals, but I'm not. Not like this. I care about them, sure. I care a lot. But what you're doing, it's reckless."

"I'm—"

"Now, listen to me." He paused, as though gathering courage before going on. "I know there's nothing I could say to change your mind. You can't say I haven't tried." He gave me a half grin. "I'm your partner and I'm going to back you up, but—"

"Oh, Dalton." I wrapped my arms around him, pinning his arms against his chest, and smacked him with a kiss on the cheek. He tried to untangle his arms and hug me back, but I quickly pulled away. What had I been thinking? I suddenly felt the need to press the wrinkles from my shirt.

"But," he said, "you need to listen to me right now. Once you're on that boat, you keep your head down. Just stick to your story. Only take the chance to place the camera if you're absolutely sure you won't get caught." He made sure I was looking at him. "Do you hear me? Absolutely sure. Then you keep your cover until you're off that boat. Do you understand? Don't do anything, and I mean anything, that will make him suspicious. Promise me."

"Helll-oooooo!" came a voice from the dock.

Dalton sighed, then turned and strode up the ladder. After a moment, he poked his head back down. "It's April." He said her name in a tone of familiarity.

"April? As in Dr. Parker, April?" She was on board and heading down the ladder before it sunk in. "What are you doing here?"

She smiled with genuine surprise. "Didn't Dalton tell you?"

He was lugging her bag in with a sheepish grin on his face. "Poppy just got back," he said to her. "Didn't have a chance yet."

Was that her suitcase?

"Oh? Well," she said, tucking her hair behind her ear and straightening to her full height. Her pants were pressed to a crisp perfection, her blouse tucked in at her tiny waist. *How does she look like she just stepped from her dressing room?* "After you left Bergen, I decided to come to our research station up here. When you called, well, Dalton and I had a nice chat." She smiled at him and he grinned back like a schoolboy. *Oh geez.* "You said you were getting on the *Forseti*, soooo, I thought maybe he could use my help."

"Well, I'm sure Special Agent Dalton is—"

"I told her that'd be great," said Dalton and set down her bag. He leaned on the ladder, his hand on his hip, looking so damn handsome, even with a swollen lip and black eye. "I could use an extra hand on board."

She nodded as if that settled it. "So it's worked out perfectly."

Yeah. Perfectly. Except Dalton could damn well manage this boat on his own. Hadn't he lectured me about involving civilians? And the way he was staring at her I thought he might need a bib.

"I'm not sure—"

"We'll be right behind you," he said. "The moment he makes contact with a killer whale, we'll have the video rolling, then I'll call the authorities and coordinate the bust."

"This is all very exciting," April said, practically in a giggle. "To be part of a Special Operation and help bring this man to justice."

Dalton blushed, all humble-like, as if she were some kind of Special Ops groupie.

"Well," she said, clasping her hands together. "I suppose I should get moved in. But if you don't mind, I'm quite thirsty."

"Oh, my gosh. Where are my manners?" said Dalton, heading for the icebox.

Oh my gosh? Seriously?

"What can I get you? Tea, coffee? We have wine."

"Water's fine, thank you." She stiffened slightly, her eyes flicking back and forth from him to me.

She must have thought I'd be gone already and they could play house.

He poured her a glass from a gallon jug, then handed it to her, gazing at her all google-eyed.

Geez. I half expected some violin music to start playing. *I gotta get out of here.* I grabbed my bag and headed for the ladder. "Okay, then. Gotta go."

"You be careful," he said to me.

I nodded. *Yeah, yeah, you're the one who*—"Wait. I still need the information about how to care for the whale. I don't want one hurt while they are trying to get it on board."

"Right," said Dr. Parker. She set down her purse, took from it a pamphlet on killer whales, and spread it open on the table. "Here," she said, pointing to a drawing of an orca, her finger on the underbelly. "Just like us, the belly is soft and vulnerable. You'll want to make sure the entire belly is supported by a sling if you try to lift one out of the water." She turned to me, her eyes on fire. "Whatever you do, don't let him raise one by the fluke."

"Okay, but I assume he knows that much. What about keeping the whale cool enough? And how do we keep it from flailing around on deck?"

She winced. "He's likely to bring them up already wrapped in a full body net. Once out of the water, you'll want to keep a close eye to make sure the body temperature doesn't go up. It averages the same as ours, about ninety-eight degrees."

"I doubt they'll have a thermometer."

"Just…make sure to constantly bathe the whale in sea water, particularly the flippers, dorsal fin, and fluke, the areas that are thin and highly vascularized."

"Vascularized? What does that mean?"

"Where the blood vessels are—"

"You know, forget it," I said. "It won't come to that." I had the tiny Go-pro mini remote camera stashed in my bag. The moment I had the footage we needed, I'd give Ray an ultimatum, tell him that if he put the whale back into the water, I'd put in a good word with the judge. There was no way I was going to let him keep a whale.

Dalton's eyebrows twitched with skepticism.

I grabbed my bag. "I need to get going." I could tell Dalton was about to pepper me with questions.

"Good luck," April said.

"Hold on," Dalton said.

Dammit.

"What did you mean, it won't come to that?"

I had to throw him a bone. "I mean, it won't come to, you

know, he's not going to quiz me on big words that he doesn't even know. I got the concept. That's what's important."

His eyebrows kept twitching.

"What?" I said, all innocent.

He spun around, a full three-sixty, his hands on the top of his head. "Poppy!"

"I'm outta here," I said and shot up the ladder.

Dalton followed me. He grabbed ahold of my arm, holding me back, controlling his breathing, trying not to explode. "Tell me you heard everything I said."

"I promised, didn't I?"

"Knowing you, you had your fingers crossed behind your back."

We stood in the cockpit in the dark for too long, staring at each other.

Finally, he muttered, "I know you're not going to—" He puffed out a lung full of air. "Just remember what I said. You know, about Michael. Be careful."

"Me? What about you?"

"What about me?"

I leaned forward and lowered my voice. "You were laying it on a bit thick down there, don't you think?"

He gave me a look of confusion.

"Don't act all innocent. You didn't have to flirt with her. She's already helping us."

"Just doing my job. Just like you."

"Aren't you the one who lectured me about involving civilians? What happened to that?"

"She's not a civilian. She's an expert informant." He grinned with satisfaction. "Do I need to remind you: we need her for *your* whole plan to work."

I averted my eyes, suddenly uncomfortable. "It's just not nice. To lead her on."

"You're the one who called her."

"Yeah, but—" I clamped my mouth shut. "Forget it."

"Poppy," he whispered, his gaze intense. "Promise me."
He looked so serious.
"Oh crap," he said, his eyes drawn over my shoulder.
I spun around. The *Forseti* was backing out of its berth.

Chapter 13

I sprinted down the dock, waving my arms like a damn fool, my pack slung over one shoulder. If the boat came close enough to the dock, I was prepared to launch like some crazy Hollywood stuntman.

The *Forseti* turned, the engine puttering along, and eased up to the fuel dock. I slowed to catch my breath. They were just fueling up tonight, before the dock staff left for the evening.

As the lines were tossed to the dockhands, I waved. Michael waved back. "I thought you were leaving without me," I said, trying to look amused rather than distraught. "Request permission to come aboard, sir."

He stepped to the side and held out his hand to help me.

Ray came pounding down the stairs from the wheelhouse, shouting orders, pointing with a cigarette clamped between two fingers. When he got to the deck, he came to a halt and eyed me up and down.

"Hello, Captain," I said. "You really should be careful walking around with—"

"Never mind that," he grumbled in my face. His breath smelled like an ashtray. He ran a hand through his greasy hair and snorked in a nose full of snot.

I suppressed a gag. Disgusting. I straightened up. "Ship's doctor, reporting for duty, sir."

"Just stay the hell out of the way."

I nodded, trying to look sheepish.

"On deck, you do what you're told."

"Yessir." *A-hole.* What I really wanted to do was wrap a fishline around his neck.

His head slowly bobbed, then he took a long drag on his cigarette, his Neanderthal eyes on me. Then when he exhaled a stream of white smoke, I had the sense he wouldn't give me another thought. *Good.*

Michael watched him walk away, waiting for him to get out of earshot, then said, "Don't mind him. He'll come around." He kissed me. "I'm glad you're here."

"Me too," I said.

I glanced around. I wanted to determine as quickly as possible where the best place to stash the remote cam might be so I could plan a midnight walk. "Do I get the grand tour of the boat?"

"Sure," he said with a shrug, as though the thought of a tour of the fishing vessel was amusing. "Drop your bag. We'll start up here." He pointed toward the bow. "Fore—" then pointed toward the back "—and aft. That's the direction on a boat,"— he winked—" in case you're told to move or something. Starboard is the right side, that is, if you're facing forward. Port is left." He gestured up the stairs. "That's the pilothouse. You won't be allowed up there." He pointed to the tall pole jutting from the top of the pilothouse like a mast with a bucket-like thing near the top. "That's the crow's nest. They climb up in there to watch for whales."

"Whales?" I said.

"Yeah," he hesitated. "They show us where the fish are."

"Oh." I nodded. That made sense, if he was really fishing anyway.

He walked aft. I followed. Behind the crow's nest, a large crane-like arm overhung the deck. The end of the fishing nets were attached to a cable that ran to it. "That's the derrick," he said. "We use it to haul in the nets."

And to haul an orca out of the sea, I bet. I looked around for a harness like Dr. Parker had described, but saw nothing.

He gestured toward a large rectangular tub. "That's the holding tank for fish." It was a tank, all right, but certainly not large enough to hold a killer whale.

He glanced around. "That's pretty much it. Ha, ha. The grand tour."

I smiled. "How do you get up in that crow's nest? It looks like fun."

He glanced up at it like it had never occurred to him to wonder. "There are rungs on the pole, I think."

If I could sneak up there, it would be an ideal place to rig the remote camera for a full, wide-angle view of the entire deck.

"Let's head in," he said and flung open the door.

I picked up my bag. He didn't notice. So much for being a gentleman.

Inside to the right was the galley, about six feet by three feet with a tiny oven and an even tinier refrigerator. To the left, a cracked laminate table sat about eight, I'd say, if they crammed in along the bench. It could have been any fishing boat on the seas for the lack of personal touches, save for an old plastic parrot that hung on a ring in the corner and an ashtray overflowing with crumpled cigarette butts wedged behind the bench and the windowsill.

To the right of the galley was a head, the door labeled with a brass plaque. Beside that, a ladder led down into the hull of the ship. "Bunks are down here." He spun around and slipped down the ladder.

I handed my bag down to him, then followed.

The berth smelled like dirty socks and wet, rubber boots. Bunks lined the hull, two on either side. The ones on top had a porthole looking out. "Bjørn sleeps in the pilothouse," Michael said. "So there's an extra bunk."

Thank goodness for cramped spaces. It'd be a lot easier to fend him off with Dylan and his father two feet away. I plopped my bag onto the empty bunk.

"Are we headed out yet this evening then?"

"No, we'll stay tied off here for the night and leave early."

"Shall we head back to the pub? Get a beer?"

"Can't." He shook his head. "My dad wants us all on board for a meeting in the galley in thirty minutes."

I tried to look disappointed but my mind went into overdrive. What would Ray tell the crew? What would he tell me now that I was on board? What did the others know?

Michael stared at me, expectant.

Then it hit me. We had thirty minutes. Alone in the bunk room. *Great.* I eased into his arms and let him kiss me. Then I pulled away. "Have I thanked you yet? I mean, this really means a lot to me." I snickered. "He won't have any idea where I've gone."

"Yeah, sure," he said, pulling me against him, his hands sliding down my back to my butt.

"I'm just saying." I grinned. I had to appeal to his gentlemanly side. And fast. "You did turn out to be my white knight."

"Uh-huh," he muttered, his lips on me again.

I pulled away again. "I just—"

He shoved me down on the bunk and ran his hand up my thigh. "Enough talk."

Crap. "My, you're in a hurry," I said, trying to sound flattered. "What's the rush?"

The door to the galley above us slammed and someone was clomping down the ladder toward us.

"Dammit. It's Dylan," Michael muttered.

Dylan came to a halt at the bottom rung, his lips pursed into a little O. His eyes flitted from me to Michael then back. "Sorry," he managed and pushed his glasses up his nose with his index finger.

Thank you, Dylan. "Maybe we should make some coffee," I suggested.

Michael glared at me. "Coffee? Right now?"

I gave him a shy, now-I'm-all-uncomfortable shrug.

His face went blank and I couldn't tell what he was thinking.

I gestured toward the galley above. "For the meeting."

He looked at Dylan with suspicion, as though debating whether he'd purposefully interrupted us. Finally, Michael shrugged and headed for the ladder without looking back.

The old helmsman, Bjørn, stared into his coffee cup, about as interested in Ray's talk as I imagined he would be in the detailed description of a colonoscopy. Dylan sat at attention. Nice young chap.

Ray sat cock-eyed on the bench, keeping his weight off his wounded ass cheek. He rolled an unlit cigarette between his yellowed fingers as he spoke. "We'll set out at oh-four-hundred on a south-southeast course, get a good distance covered before daybreak." He lit the cigarette, then said through the smoke as he shook out the match, "I've gotten word the fishing should be good around here"—he ran his fingers along a chart, laying out the path we'd be traveling—"maybe day after tomorrow. I want to get as far south as we can."

Yep, right where Dr. Parker said the K-pod would be.

Michael added, "Fuel is topped off. Supplies on board. We're good to go."

Ray nodded in acknowledgment. "Bjørn, you can sleep in. Dylan and I will take the first shift."

Dylan's eyebrows shot up with surprise. Obviously, this was an uncommon occurrence. "But I'm—"

Ray glared at Dylan, who snapped his mouth shut. "Once we're out of the harbor and have a course set, you can get to work on breakfast."

"Roi, sir," Dylan said, forcing his cheer.

"Bjørn and Michael will take the evening shift. We're not stopping until we find what we're looking for."

"And what about me, sir?" I asked.

"What about you?" he said as he ground out the stub of his cigarette without even a glance my way.

"How can I help?"

He reached for another cigarette. "Stay out of the way."

I looked to Michael, who averted his eyes.

Ray said. "When we launch the nets, I don't want you out on deck. You stay inside. Got it?"

"Oh?" I said. *Crap.* "I'm sure I can lend a hand. I'm stronger than I look."

"It's for your own safety," Michael said with a dismissive shrug. "Deep water fishing is dangerous work."

I swear I saw Bjørn hide a harrumph. I wasn't sure if it was on account of the danger of fishing or because he knew there'd be no fishing. He was hard to read.

Ray sat back, a smug grin on his face. "All goes as planned, and Christmas'll come early this year, boys."

I smiled—a big, fat naive smile. *We'll see about that.*

Chapter 14

If Bjørn slept in the wheelhouse, it would be difficult to get up and into the crow's nest without him hearing me. I needed an excuse. Preferably for a time when no one would be watching and see me mount the camera. But what excuse and when?

I lay in the bunk listening to Ray snore. Every exhalation gave me visions of the roof peeling back like the lid of a sardine can, then rolling back up when he inhaled. How can a man breathe like that, anyway?

Michael was asleep in the bunk opposite his, oblivious.

Dylan, in the bunk next to me, slept with his legs pulled up to his chest, curled up into a ball, blankets swirled into a nest. Like a baby hedgehog. I grinned. I had no clue how to take the temperature of a hedgehog. Good thing Michael hadn't asked.

I had no idea how to take the temperature of an orca either. Not that it mattered. I wasn't going to let it get that far. I needed to allow Ray to do what he was going to do, to get one in the sling if I had to, but there was no way he was getting one on board and keeping it. Not if I could help it.

Sure, Dalton might get close enough in the *Sea Mist* to get the video evidence we needed for a court trial months from now, assuming the Norwegian authorities would do their part and arrest him, at some point, but what if they didn't? What would happen to the whale? I had to stop him myself. I had to find a way to get the video *and* sabotage the whole damn operation.

I had to find it fast.

There was no reason I could think of to be in the crow's nest tonight. It was too risky. Sleep was what I needed. Then tomorrow, I'd figure out what to do.

The engines rumbled to life and I sat up in my bunk. I hadn't heard Ray leave the cabin. *Damn.* What the hell kind of agent was I?

My watch read four a.m. At least Ray was punctual.

There wasn't a thing I could do right now but go back to sleep, get it while I could. I lay back down and stared at the bunk above me. *One sugar plum fairy. Two sugar plum fairies.* Nope. Wasn't going to work. And I'd really rather not be alone with Michael in the bunk room. Might as well get up.

I crept into the head, washed my face, and pulled my hair into a ponytail. I patted the remote cam that was stuffed in my jacket pocket to be sure it was there before I went topside.

Dylan was on deck, manning the lines while we pulled away from the dock.

Dalton had anticipated our departure. The *Sea Mist* was gone from her slip.

With April on board. I crossed my arms, Dalton's voice in my head, *I told her that'd be great. I could use an extra hand.* Geez.

I wasn't sure where to go. Michael had said I wouldn't be allowed in the wheelhouse. Perhaps I needed to ingratiate myself to old Ray.

I slipped into the galley and rifled through the cupboards. I found the coffee pot and coffee. That ought to do the trick.

Ten minutes later I knocked on the door to the wheelhouse, cups in hand. "Coffee?" I said with a sweet, innocent smile.

Dylan smiled back. Ray grumbled something indiscernible.

I took it as a welcome and strode in and handed each of them a cup.

Ray didn't make any noise like I should get out, so I eased onto the bench, watched out the windows as we left the harbor, and kept my mouth shut, hoping he'd forget I was there.

I liked being in the pilothouse. All four walls were windows so I could see in any direction. It was too dark to see the *Sea Mist*, though. But sure as the sun, Dalton was out here somewhere.

By the time we'd cleared the harbor and turned south, Ray'd smoked his third cigarette and I was starting to feel green. I needed out of here. I needed fresh air.

I held up Ray's empty coffee mug. "More coffee?"

"Dylan'll get it," he said, a command, not a suggestion.

"O…K," I said.

Ray kept his eyes forward as Dylan took his cue and slipped out, mugs in hand.

The door clicked shut and the air in the roomed seemed even more oppressive—sharp and metallic smelling. The darkness felt like a blanket over the windshield, the eerie glow of the instruments the only light. The low rumble of the engine seemed to mask every other sound.

Ray didn't turn or even look at me as, in a low tone, he said, "Why are you on my boat?"

The hairs on the back of my neck stood up. "I don't understand," I said with a shrug. "I thought you wanted me to keep an eye on your—"

"And here you are," he said. He eased back in the chair, a deliberate move, and tilted his head to look at me. The greenish reflection on the surface of his eyes made him look ghoulish.

I drew in a quick breath and my eyes dropped to his hands. He drew his fingers into tight fists, then flexed them and picked up a length of rope that Dylan had been using to practice knot tying.

"I meant, what are you really doing here?" He turned and

looked at me with a blank expression, his entire body held taut save for his rough, tar-stained fingers, testing the strength of the rope.

"Well, I…" *Stick to the story.* "My boyfriend, well, he turned out to be a real ass."

His eyes narrowed. "And why's that my problem?"

The hands clenched the rope, slowly twisting the end around one hand, working it like he was working out my story, turning it over in his mind. He switched hands, wrapping the end around his left hand.

"I planned to leave on the ferry, but Michael seemed…well, I liked him—"

"That so?" he said. His right hand gripped the rope and snapped it tight.

"Well, I admit, when we met, I'd kinda hoped—"

"You know what we do on this boat?"

"You fish?" I said with a shrug as if I had no idea what he was getting at.

"We work." He held up the rope, examining it as if it were some kind of clairvoyance-inducing object, then his eyes settled on me. "We work hard. Ain't no room for girly drama."

"Yessir," I said. "I can work hard. You wait and see. I won't disappoint."

His expression turned to one of amused contemplation, as if he thought what I'd said was funny.

The door creaked open and Dylan strolled in, mugs in hand, his cheerful presence like a gust of fresh air.

Ray tossed the bit of rope onto the console and rose to take a cup.

"I think I'll watch the sun rise from the deck," I said, escaping the room.

Ray grunted and turned his back on me. Dylan watched me go with a look of confusion.

On the bow, the crisp morning air whipped my hair against my face and chilled my ears. I worked to get my breathing back to normal.

Michael came up behind me. "You were up early," he said. A statement that felt like an accusation.

"I couldn't sleep. New bed. New noises."

"Well, you shouldn't wander around the boat by yourself." He wrapped his arms around me, pinning my arms at my sides, and it took all my will power not to break from his embrace. "It's not safe," he said. "A fishing boat has so many hazards. You could easily trip and fall overboard." He squeezed me tighter and added, "No one would even know you were missing."

A shiver ran through me, but it wasn't from the cold. I tried to shake it off. I was just a girl who left her boyfriend and ran off with a fisherman. Nothing to worry about.

As we stood at the rail, his arms around me, the light blue sky in the east turned to pink, then orange rimmed the edges of the peaks on the horizon. A muted reflection of it all shimmered on the ocean's surface. Ray had been right. The storm had passed earlier than predicted. Wispy clouds stretched across the sky.

"Looks like cotton candy," I said, trying to keep it light.

"You're right," Michael said. "I don't usually pay much attention to the sights."

It was an opening. I had a job to do. "Ooooh, I hope we see whales," I said. "What do you think?"

His arms tensed. "Possible," he said.

I swiveled within his embrace, facing him now, and pointed to the crow's nest. "From up there, right?"

He craned his neck to see. "Yeah, I guess."

"Didn't you say you watch for whales from up there?"

"Yeah, well, I meant in the old days." He hugged me tighter. "Aren't you cold?"

"Yeah, kinda." I sighed. "I think it's romantic. How the ancient mariners would set out on the ocean, sometimes for months at a time, on a whale hunt. What an adventure. Wouldn't that be exciting?"

He didn't flinch. He leaned forward and nuzzled my neck.

"Uh-huh."

I spun around. "You're right. I'm cold. Let's go back inside."

I gave him a quick peck on the lips. *Now, get your hands off me.*

I needed to get this job done fast and get the hell off this boat.

The best time to get up in the crow's nest would be when Ray and Michael were both down below. After dark would be ideal. Ray might turn in early since he'd been up before dawn. That is, if we didn't get to the killer whales first. But Michael had the late shift. I'd keep my fingers crossed.

After lunch, during which Ray had said a total of seven words, especially nothing about the proximity of the whales, I went back out on deck. The fine mist in the air clung to my face, soft and cool. I glanced back and caught sight of the *Sea Mist,* tucked in a cove. *Good.* Dalton was lying low.

The *Forseti* puttered along the coast of jagged granite mountains, the slopes covered in a velvety-green carpet, their peaks dusted with a fresh layer of white snow. I breathed in deeply, the crisp sea air filling me with calm. Such beauty, all around us. And men like Ray, all they can see is money. The mountains, the trees, the waterfalls, the sea, the whales. All for the taking. The plunder to those who would be bold enough, strong enough. With no regard for anyone else, any other being.

It seemed a sad state of living. With no reverence. No appreciation.

The Buddha would have me pity Ray. But truly, I wanted to wrap my hands around his neck and squeeze. He reminded me of a troll like those who lived in these mountains—curmudgeonly creatures, short and stout with bulbous noses and bushy eyebrows. Under the cover of darkness, they spirit away beautiful maidens, tucking them in their mountain lairs, forcing them to spin by day and scratch the trolls' heads by night. Gift shops in Bergen were stuffed full of all renditions of them, from the cutesy to the obscene.

Fantastical trolls fueled my imagination as a child, but I was more interested now in the real creatures that inhabited this land. I was content to watch, waiting for a glimpse of one, then sure enough, off the starboard bow I caught sight of something in the water. Then it was gone. I kept my eyes where I had seen it and a gray head popped up again. Big round eyes set in a bulbous head, whiskers like a dog's. A harbor seal.

He disappeared below the surface again. But for a moment, I'd seen him and he'd seen me.

"That your boyfriend back there?" I spun around. Ray stood behind me, his Cro-Magnon stare fixed on me. Michael hovered behind him.

The *Sea Mist* puttered along now, following not far behind. *Damn.*

"What? Boyfriend? I don't have a boyfriend."

Ray handed me a pair of binoculars and gestured aft with his cigarette. "That him following us or not?"

I raised the binoculars. Dalton was at the helm, April standing next to him. Did he have his arm around her? "Yeah, maybe, I don't know."

Ray took a long drag from his cigarette, looking at me with suspicious eyes.

"He can chase me if he wants. I'm not going back to him." I smiled at Michael, all flirty. "Not now." I felt like I should be chewing on a mouth full of gum, maybe tug a strand out and wrap it around my finger for the full effect.

Ray grumbled something to Michael and climbed the stairs to the wheelhouse.

"What are you doing out here?" Michael asked. "I thought I told you to stay inside." His stare said it all. The bottom dropped out of my stomach.

"Yeah," I said. "Sorry. I just needed a quick breath of fresh air."

His expression didn't change.

"It's cold out here anyway. I was thinking of making some coffee," I said, trying to act as though I was used to being talked to like that. "Should be ready in ten minutes or so if you want some." I headed for the galley, hoping he wouldn't follow.

Dylan was at the sink, earbuds in his ears, his hands plunged into a tiny mountain of soap suds. He was humming along to the tune, oblivious to my entrance.

"Can I help you with those?" I asked, moving into his peripheral vision.

"Huh?" he said, startled. He yanked the earbuds from his ears, splattering suds down the front of his sweatshirt.

"The dishes," I said. "Can I help?"

"Uh, sure." He handed me a dish towel. "Yer can dry."

I took care of the plates, then the cups, listening to the Irish band blasting from the tiny speakers now dangling from Dylan's neck. How could he abuse his eardrums like that?

"So what made you want to be a fisherman?" I asked.

"Does anyone *want* ter be a fisherman?" he said with a grin, then shrugged. "De pay is gran'." He handed me a freshly scrubbed and rinsed saucepan.

"You grew up in Ireland, right? By the sea? Was your dad a fisherman?"

Dylan's light complexion turned pink. "Naw, naw. Oi jist wanted ter git away, 'av an adventure, oi guess."

"And has it been? An adventure?"

"It's been lashings av derdy dishes, I'll tell yer dat."

He pulled the drain plug and rinsed the sink clean while I tucked the dish rack into a cupboard.

"Wanna play Cribbage?" he asked without much enthusiasm, as though he assumed I'd say no.

"Sure," I said.

A brief flicker of surprise crossed his face before he composed himself. He flung open a drawer and tossed a deck of cards on the table.

"You don't have other work to do?" I asked.

"Not 'til dinner." He shuffled the cards. "Unless they fend a school av cod. But they won't," he said, matter-of-fact.

"What do you mean?"

He glanced toward the door, then leaned forward and whispered, "They're not pure gran' at it."

"Fishing, you mean?"

He nodded. "I've been wi' dem nigh for foive weeks. 'aven't dropped a net."

"Maybe the herring are late this year," I said.

He shook his head. "Oi asked in town." A grin spread across his face. His eyebrows raised, he said, "At laest 'e's payin' me."

"What are you saying, Dylan? You think something is fishy?" I snickered at my own joke. Trying to keep it light.

He stared at me for a long, drawn-out moment. I wasn't sure if he was going to respond. Then he made the slightest nod.

I whispered, "What do you think's going on?"

The door swung open and Michael came in with a gust of cold air. *Damn.*

"Coffee ready?" His eyes searched the stove, then the countertop, as if the coffee pot might be lurking in some mysterious corner.

"No, I ended up helping with the dishes." I gave him an innocent smile. "Warmed me up."

"Uh-huh," he said, his eyes shifting from me to Dylan. He was trying to catch me in a lie. I wondered what he'd do when he did. Dalton following in the *Sea Mist* wasn't helping. It had put Michael even more on edge with me. "Well, make some, will ya?"

"Sure," I said and got up from the table.

Michael left, slamming the door behind him.

Dylan raised his eyebrows but said nothing.

After I set the pot to percolate, I sat back down with Dylan. "He's probably annoyed because my boyfriend, I mean, my ex-boyfriend is following us. Like he won't let me go and he's chasing after me or something. Can you believe that?"

"Yeah," he said without looking at me. "If yer were me lassy, oi nu oi wud."

I paused. *How sweet.* "He's already got another girl." *April.* April with the pretty blond hair and the Ph.D. "She's on board with him."

He looked me in the eyes and grinned. "Well, dat seems ter 'av put a bee in yisser bonnet."

I crossed my arms. "Not at all. He and I are through."

"Gran'." He shuffled the cards some more and dealt.

I kept a crappy hand and tossed a ten and a five in his crib. Dylan might end up being an ally, but it would serve me that he and everyone else on board think I was an airhead.

"De coffee's ready," he said.

"I'll take it," I said and went to play waitress to a wildlife thief and his son while I tried to figure out how the hell I was going to plant my video camera.

CHAPTER 15

After dinner, the darkness had already returned. The slow forward momentum of the boat moving through the water was making me drowsy. Nothing had been spotted. Thankfully. Because I still hadn't found a way to get up to the crow's nest and plant the camera.

Ray and Michael pored over charts at the dining table in the galley. Bjørn was in the wheelhouse alone.

"I'm going to see if Bjørn needs anything," I said and got up and left.

I circled the deck once, debating if I could get up the ladder without Bjørn hearing me. Probably not. Maybe I could give him a reason. I circled once more, then climbed the stairs and poked my head in through the door to the pilothouse. "May I join you?"

"Don't see why not," Bjørn said, a hint of wariness in his posture.

I took my perch on the bench. "Thanks."

A greenish-blue glow from the monitors lit the old man's face as he looked out at the sea, his eyes moving in a slow, steady scanning pace along the horizon, then to the chart plotter, then to the radar screen, then back out the front window. In his hand he held a dirty coffee mug, the rim chipped in three places, the logo long since rubbed off.

"How long have you been a captain?" I asked.

"Helmsman," he said, as though the distinction were quite important.

"Helmsman then."

He hesitated before he answered. "I could steer a boat as soon as I was tall enough to reach the wheel, if that's what yer asking."

"And fishing?"

He turned to look at me with tired eyes. "I'm Norwegian. It's in my blood."

I sensed I'd irritate him if I talked too much, so I held back, listened to the silence for a while.

Bjørn set his cup down on the console and leaned back in the chair. Something about him seemed perfectly at home, as if he were part of the boat itself. Suddenly I realized why. This *was* his boat. Ray hadn't hired him to come on as helmsman; he'd hired the whole kit and caboodle. I wondered if Bjørn knew what he'd signed up for. Maybe he was desperate for cash. Or maybe he was as ruthless a criminal as Ray.

Watching him closely for any kind of reaction, I asked, "You see whales often?"

He slowly turned and looked at me, his lips pursed, crinkles at the edges of his sharp, blue eyes, all so subtle, if I hadn't been looking for it, I might not have noticed. He raised the mug of coffee. Took a sip. "Yeah."

"I'd love to see a whale," I said, easily conjuring the excited anticipation of my twelve-year-old self. "I hear there are humpbacks and killer whales in these seas."

He nodded, his eyes shifting back to his monitors. "Yep."

"Do you think we'll see any?"

His eyes came back to me, measuring. "Could."

"I'm going to keep watch," I said.

The coffee cup was raised to his lips again as he scanned the horizon, then the monitors. Bjørn didn't strike me as the kind of man who got rattled easily. They say deep sea fishing is one of the most dangerous jobs on the planet. I suppose if you spend a lifetime doing something like that, staring death in the face every time you go out, everything else seems trivial.

If he didn't want to, he wasn't going to give up any hints as to what he knew, how much he'd been told, what he'd agree to, or what he'd surmised on his own. This man was a closed book.

"Michael says that's what the crow's nest is for. To watch for whales. You ever been up there?"

Bjørn grinned. The first I'd seen. "When I was a boy. It was my job."

"Really?" Maybe I could get him talking after all. "Was your father a whaler then?"

"My father. My grandfather. My great-grandfather before him."

"And you were the spotter? How young were you?"

"Oh, I started at six or seven. When I was old enough to see over the rail."

"I bet it was exciting." *Not to mention horrific.*

"It was work. Not much else." He looked at me. His eyes soft. "Why you asking so many questions?"

I shrugged. "Bored, I guess." I chewed on my fingernail. Time for some pointless questions. "How do you live out here, anyway, day after day? Nothing but blue on blue."

He chuckled. "I suppose you'd see it that way."

"What do you mean?"

"It's a way of life. It's part of who I am." He looked out at the dark sea and I sensed a weariness in his manner. "It's what it means to live in the north."

"Fishing and whaling, you mean?"

"Blue on blue, as you say."

I waited a few minutes, to not seem too eager, before I asked, "Do you have any children?"

"A son," he said, the thought taking him far away.

"Is he a whaler, too?"

He retreated into his cup of coffee for a time, then said, "No money in it." He sighed. "My boy works on an oil rig in the south."

"That because the whales are going extinct?"

He smirked. "It's the whalers that are going extinct."

"Oh?" I had to tread carefully. "What do you mean?"

"Politics." He adjusted something on the plotter, then turned to me. "Easy for some rich kid from the continent, sitting in a Starbucks, sipping on a chocolate latte, or whatever dey call dose over-priced coffee drinks, plunking at keys on a computer all day, buying and selling electronics or oil or vatever he can make money at, vearing some fancy suit." He picked up his coffee mug again but kept talking, his accent really pronounced. "His vife buys 'is dinner some time between nine and five at a store with fluorescent lights, a slab of someting shrink-wrapped to a sheet of styrofoam." He gave me a sharp look. "Don't look at me like dat, like I'm some raving lunatic. I ain't saying it's right. I'm saying that fool ain't got de right to judge me is all." He shook his finger. "Dat ain't tofu he's eating. Ask a man who lives hand to mouth, trying to feed a hungry family, living in a land like dis. Ask him what he thinks of killing a whale."

I wasn't sure if I was in more awe of the content of his rant or the fact that he'd said so many words at once. But I was sure that, somewhere in there, he'd said it wasn't right.

He drained the last of his coffee. "I don't know what I'm going on about. It don't matter no how."

"What do you mean, it doesn't matter?"

"I mean, the cost of hunting whales is high, returns are low. Supply and demand. Nobody eats whale meat anymore." He smirked. "They're living on chocolate lattes."

"Well, I know one thing."

"What's that, little lady?"

"Now I'm craving chocolate."

He grinned.

We sat together for a while. It was comfortable. I liked

Bjørn. He seemed kind and gentle. Not the evil whaler of the tabloids. This man knew what it meant to live by one's means, to work hard. He had convictions. They might not match mine, but they were there just the same. I suspected he wasn't fond of Ray Goldman.

Ray came into the wheelhouse and told Bjørn he wanted him to anchor for the night. And I saw it. Subtle. Bjørn's eyes gave him away. I was right. He didn't like Ray much. He didn't like him much at all.

Michael stepped into the room, took me by the hand, and led me out. "We're anchoring so we might as well turn in," he said. "Big day tomorrow."

"Oh?" I said.

"We think we've found fish."

On the other side of the door, Bjørn and Ray were hashing something out. Their tone revealed an argument, but I couldn't make out the words.

"I think I'll stay up for a bit longer," I said.

"Aren't you tired?"

"Nah," I said. "Besides, Bjørn and I were having an interesting conversation." *And I have a camera to stash.*

Michael looked through the window toward Bjørn with an expression of confused suspicion. "That old man?"

I shrugged. "What can I say? I like his fish tales."

Ray flung open the door and pushed past us without a word.

Michael lingered for a moment as though pondering what might come of me staying with Bjørn before he shrugged and followed.

"I won't be long," I said. I breathed in deeply. This was my chance.

Bjørn gave no hint of his disagreement with Ray and a half hour later, I'd been lulled into a sleepy daze by the chug-chug-chug of the engine and the warmth of too many electronics, when Bjørn brought the boat to a halt, the hook was dropped, and the engine went quiet.

"Look at that," Bjørn said and pointed at the sky through the window.

I ducked to see. "Is that—"

"Go out on deck."

I raced to the bow. The night sky shimmered with strands of green. The aurora borealis. Light pulsed in vertical ribbons, like a giant drape of chiffon moving in a gentle breeze. Green shafts with tips of red against a black velvety sky pocked with millions of sparkling stars. No wonder primitive peoples stood in awe of the mystery. Like dancing spirits, moving through the heavens, casting a green glow across the snow-capped mountain peaks. I'd never seen anything like it.

Bjørn, standing beside me, his voice low, said, "Some say it is the spirits of old maids, dancing in the sky. Others say it is the Valkyries, the immortal, female warriors of legend. Ravens by the light of day; by night, they carry spears and armor that glow in the dark sky." His voice changed to a low, reverent tone. "In battle, they are the ones who decide who lives and who dies."

"Are you saying it's some kind of omen?"

"I'm saying some things are better left to the gods."

I stared at the awe-inspiring light show before me. Is that how life should be? Leave everything to the gods? Should I let them decide the fate of the whales? Nope. I would decide. "They didn't make capricious decisions, though, right?" I said. "I always thought they were the goddesses of vengeance and retribution."

He smirked. "You're all right, you know that?"

I nodded. This was my chance. My chance to get up to the crow's nest and mount the camera. But how could I do it without him watching? Would he tell Ray I'd been up there?

I let my eyes travel to the top. It wasn't going to be a quick and easy climb. The danger lay in the time it would take to get up there and back down again. If Ray or Michael happened back on deck and caught me, their suspicions would launch into the stratosphere.

If I got caught up there, and they found the camera, it'd be the end.

"I bet the view is spectacular from up in that crow's nest. Mind if I give it a try?"

His tired eyes rose about halfway up the post. "That is where a raven would go," he mumbled and went back into the wheelhouse.

Hand over hand, I climbed the pole toward the crow's nest. The steel rungs were ice cold, but I moved quickly, afraid my clammy hands might stick. I flipped myself up and over the edge of the bucket and inside. I popped up and scanned the deck for Ray or Michael. It was too dark to see a damn thing. One of them could be standing there watching me right now and I wouldn't know it. Well. This was my only chance. It was now or never.

The bucket had a rim all around, but nothing onto which I could attach the camera. It would have to go under the bucket, on the bracket there.

As fast as I could, I climbed back out of the perch, scrambled down a few rungs, and, as I held on with one hand, took the camera from my pocket with the other. I scanned the deck again, from one side to the other for movement. Still couldn't see anything. If anyone was watching, there would be no doubt what I was up to. What I wouldn't give for a pair of night-vision goggles right now. I took a deep breath and tried to stop my hand from shaking.

I clipped the remote cam to the bracket, checked again to make sure I wasn't being watched, pointless as it was, then reached back up and angled it toward the aft deck. I couldn't check the view without my laptop, so I had to get it right the first time. There was no way I was going to get a chance to climb up here again. My best guess on the angle would have to do.

I backed down the pole, then went down the stairs and circled the deck to be sure no one had seen me. With a sigh of relief, I said a silent prayer to the Valkyries that no one would look up and see it, then climbed the stairs and slipped back into the wheelhouse. "Whew, too cold for that," I said. "I don't know what I was thinking."

He gave me an amused nod.

CHAPTER 16

Bjørn turned in for bed. I went into the galley and rifled through the cupboards for chocolate. You'd think they'd at least have an Oreo cookie or something on board.

I sat down at the table empty-handed and confessed to myself. I was scared. Scared shitless, actually. All they had to do was look up and they'd see it and then…

If I got lucky, and they kept their eyes from the pole, I'd get what I came for. But video footage was one thing. I had to do more. Scared or not, I needed to figure out a way to keep Ray from getting a killer whale on board at all. If he got one in a net, that was enough to convict, but if he got one on board, it would be life threatening for the whale. Dr. Parker had said its chances weren't good, especially if Ray didn't know what he was doing.

A harness would be attached to the winch arm to haul the orca on board. That was the key. That's what I had to take out of the equation. The harness. But where was it?

Dalton had said to do nothing else, to keep my head down. But how could I stand by and do nothing?

I checked my phone. There was actually one bar of service out here. I shot off a text to Dalton.

Poppy: You there?

I waited. Nothing. Maybe he didn't have service where he was anchored. I leaned back and tried to picture the layout of the deck. The harness must be made of canvas, or plastic maybe.

My phone buzzed.

Dalton: Yep. You ok?

Poppy: Fine. Camera's in place.

Dalton: Good. Sit tight.

Poppy: You're pushing my cover. You need to stay back.

But not too far.

Dalton: What happened?

Poppy: Just don't push it.

Dalton: Poppy, what's going on?

Poppy: Nothing. Everything is fine.

I can handle it.

Dalton: Just stick to your cover story and hold tight.

I can't. I've got to stop him.

Poppy: Yep.

Dalton: Everything ok with Michael?

Poppy: Fine.

Dalton: Are you sure? I can still get you off that boat. Say the word.

Poppy: Just trust me already.

Nothing.

Poppy: Gotta go.

I clicked off and deleted all the texts in case Ray checked my phone. I took a deep breath. I had work to do.

The boat gently rose and fell on the waves, the fishing gear creaking and clanking with the rocking. Hopefully, any noise I might make would blend in with the ruckus and no one would notice.

My guess was that the lazarettes with the padlocks were the ones with the harness and other whale-hauling gear, but I had to check anyway. I started on the side of the boat opposite where I'd already checked back in the harbor.

Again, on this side as well, the first one was padlocked. I stepped lightly, moving to the next one. No padlock. I lifted the lid a few inches and peeked inside. This was it. The harness. I was sure of it. What luck! I eased the lid back and clipped it to the rail to keep it open.

Clank-clank-clank came footsteps down the stairs. *Crap*. A dose of adrenaline shot into my bloodstream. I clicked off my flashlight and ducked beside the bin. Bjørn must have been going to the head. The door to the galley swung open and the light clicked on. I waited, unable to hear anything over the lapping of the waves against the hull and my heart thumping in my chest.

A few minutes passed and he didn't come back out. If he woke anyone down below and they noticed I wasn't in my bunk, I'd be screwed. I needed to come up with a good reason for being on deck, and quick.

More time passed and he still didn't emerge. What was he doing in there? I crept from my hiding spot to peek in the window. Bjørn was at the stove setting a teakettle to boil. *Damn*. My crappy luck. He was probably a world-record-setting insomniac. What if he sat at the table doing crosswords or writing letters to his wife back home for half the night? All I could do was wait him out. I couldn't head to bed now, having to pass through to below decks without an explanation.

Back to my hiding spot I went to wait. I had no coat and the night was freezing cold. *Bad planning, McVie.* I considered crawling under the nets to get warm, but that made me think of Dalton and his body snuggled up against me. And how I'd smell like rotten fish.

Finally, my lips blue and my hands too cold to work properly, I heard the clank-clank-clank of footsteps on the iron stairs as Bjørn headed back up to the pilothouse.

As soon as the door banged shut, I slipped from behind the

lazarrette and shined my flashlight inside. The harness had two poles with a canvas sling attached, a basic home-made contraption. If I could cut the sling where it attached to the poles, I could weaken it. When the orca was being lifted from the water, the canvas would rip.

I started to unroll it when I realized that wouldn't work. What if they had the whale high in the air, or worse yet, over the deck, and it came slamming down? I needed to render it completely unusable.

With my pocket knife, I could saw at the roping, cut the canvas to bits. That would do it. But then, when Ray saw it, he'd know it had been purposefully sabotaged. Too risky.

The best option was to tangle its cords, rip the canvas in a way that looked like it had happened when it was put in the bin. I lifted one end of the harness and started to rewrap the cords when the hinge of the galley door creaked. I froze. Someone was out on deck. I shoved the harness back in the lazarette.

"Poppy?" It was Michael.

I threw down the flashlight, sending it rolling across the deck to distract him and eased the lid down. "You startled me," I said, my heart going zippity-zap.

He picked up the flashlight. "What are you doing out here?" he said, his tone accusatory.

"I couldn't sleep." *Crap.* "I was feeling kinda cooped up, you know. Needed to walk." *Did he see me close the lid?*

"What did I tell you about being out on the deck alone?" I couldn't read his expression in the dark, but his arms were crossed and his stance was threatening.

"Well, I figured since we were anchored—"

"Oh, you figured, did you?" He put his arm around me, pulling me toward him with a powerful grip. "Well, darlin', it's going to be a long journey if you can't get a handle on this cabin fever."

"I'll be all right," I said, hoping he couldn't feel my pulse racing into oblivion. "I'm sorry. I didn't mean to worry you."

"C'mon back to bed and try it again," he said, his tone softened. "After this cold air, you'll get toasty warm and fall right to sleep. I promise."

I nodded. I was plenty warm now, what with my nerves set on fire. Maybe I should have had Dalton pick me up. *No. The job isn't finished.* I could handle this. But I couldn't think of any excuse Michael'd accept for me to stay out here alone now. And if he caught me sneaking up here again, that'd be the end. *Dammit!*

Reluctantly, I followed Michael back down to the bunks. I'd have to think of something else. Before they found the whales.

Chapter 17

The engines roared to life and I sat up so fast I knocked my head on the bunk above me. My watch read 7:30. Ray's bunk was empty.

Then the clank-clank-clank of the anchor being raised echoed through the hull. Had Ray got word that whales were nearby?

I got dressed, clipped the camera remote inside my jacket pocket, and went topside.

Ray and Michael were in the pilothouse. Making coffee had gotten me in there yesterday. *Let's see if it will work again.*

I brewed a pot, poured mugs, and knocked at the door.

Ray's scowl burned through the window. I smiled wide, acting like I didn't notice. "Coffee?"

Michael ambled over to the door and took the mugs from me. "Thanks."

Ray gripped the edge of the door. "We're busy," he grumbled and pushed it shut in my face.

Damn. Must be I was right. Orcas are close.

I shot off a quick text to Dalton.

Poppy: You up? We're on the move.

I waited. No answer. I checked again. The one reception bar flickered and went out.

I paced around in the galley dining room, glancing out the window every eight seconds. The sky to the east was a light blue. We were moving through the water at what I assumed was full throttle for this vessel. Pans and plates rattled in the cupboards. The plastic parrot swung back and forth on the ring. I pressed against the window, searching the dark sea for a glimpse of an orca, the other direction for Dalton. Nothing either way.

Might as well make something to eat. I found eggs, milk, and flour, whipped them together, poured the batter into a high-sided pan, slid it into the oven, then paced some more.

About twenty minutes later, Dylan stumbled in, one eye open. "Dat coffee oi peggy dell?"

"There's probably a cup left in the pot."

"Mercy," he said.

"I've got a German pancake in the oven."

He looked my way and opened the other eye. "Tryin' ter take my job?"

"No, sir," I said with a grin.

He poured the mug of coffee and slumped down at the table. "Must be 'e's finally foun' sum cod."

"Why do you say that?"

Dylan shrugged. "We're actually movin'."

"Does that mean we'll have fish for dinner?" I asked.

"Oi wouldn't play dohs odds," he said.

I wondered again if he really didn't know what was going on. He seemed so genuine, it was hard to believe he did. "Do you think maybe we're not out here for fish but something else?"

"Loike waaat?" he asked, his expression pure ignorance. "Mermaids?"

The door opened and Ray poked his head in. "I need to talk to you. Outside."

I looked to Dylan, then back to Ray. He was staring at me. My stomach lurched. If he'd seen the camera, I was done for. "Me?"

"You," he said and shut the door.

Dylan and I exchanged a what-the-hell-is-that-about look before I got up and followed Ray out the door.

When I stepped on deck, Ray pointed aft. "He's still following us."

Dalton. A surge of relief flooded me. "What? Who? No way."

Ray fished a battered pack of Marlboros from his coat pocket, whacked it until a cigarette emerged from the opening, then shoved the stick of chemically-soaked tobacco into his mouth. He cupped a lit match in his hands to block the wind and took a long drag before he said, "I want him gone." When I didn't react, he leaned forward, smoke oozing from his nose and mouth. "Now."

"Well, I'm sure he's just out—"

"I'm not going to tell you twice."

I believe you. I opened my hands and gave him an innocent shrug. "What do you want me to do about it?"

"You'll think of something." He flashed a condescending frown. "Or I'll throw you overboard to give him something to do."

His expression didn't change. He wasn't kidding.

I swallowed hard. "Can I use the radio?"

He held out his hand, mocking a cordial, be-my-guest gesture.

In the wheelhouse, I took the transmitter in hand and held down the button. "*Sea Mist, Sea Mist, Sea Mist*, this is the *Forseti* hailing. Over."

"*Forseti*, this is *Sea Mist*, switch to channel 68. Over."

I turned the tuning dial to 68 and heard Dalton's voice. "*Forseti*, this is *Sea Mist*."

"Yeah, *Sea Mist*, uh, you need to divert your course."

"Come again?"

"Stop following us." Dalton was smart enough to know I wouldn't be calling on the radio if I wasn't being watched. He'd know to play along.

"What is it they say, hell hath no fury like a woman scorned? Ha ha. Get over yourself, sweetheart. We aren't following you. You happen to be on our course."

I shook my head. *Good Dalton, keep it up.* "Whatever. Just choose another course."

"What? I will not. You don't get to tell me where to go."

Ray was hovering like a vulture over a kill, his beady eyes fixed on me. Michael stood behind him, arms crossed.

"It's over. There's no point in chasing me," I said. "I'm not coming back."

"Chasing you? Very funny." There was a click and a second of static. "Our days are over, babe."

"Good, then just turn around. Go another way."

"No can do. Over and out."

I turned to Ray and shrugged.

He curled up his lip as though he'd just got a whiff of rotting carcass. "Come with me," he said and grabbed me by the wrist.

"All right, I'm coming," I said. *What the hell?*

He stomped down the stairs and headed toward the stern, to one of the lazarettes on the port side. The one with the harness inside. My pulse started thrumming, my brain whirring with excuses, denials. He opened the lid, looked inside, and slammed it shut. He moved back to the one with a padlock on it and fished a key from his back pocket, opened the lock, and flipped open the lid. "Take a look," he said.

I leaned over the side, making it clear I was obeying. There was an army green case with Russian writing on the side—the case for a rocket-propelled grenade launcher. *Oh crap.* My knees went numb. "What is it?" I asked as innocently as I could muster.

Ray reached down and flipped open the lid to reveal the weapon. "It's proof that I'm not talking out my ass. You don't get your boyfriend to back off, I will." He slammed the lid shut and the latch rattled, echoing in my brain.

"Right," I said, my eyes wide. "I'll convince him."

Apparently Ray wasn't concerned at this point about what I knew. *Not good.* I went straight back to the wheelhouse. Ray didn't follow me, but I had the feeling he would be listening. I hailed Dalton again. "Listen, my captain won't take no for an answer. He wants you out of our fishing area."

"What does he care? I'm not fishing."

"Well, he's a little hot-headed. Just leave, okay. Don't make me thump you on the head."

Bjørn gave me a curious look. There was no response from Dalton for a moment. I hoped he would pick up on my hint. In the Navy, grenade launchers were nicknamed thumpers and hot meant firepower.

"Fine. Whatever," he finally responded. "Have a great life."

"I'm set on the course I want to be. You need to find yours."

There was no answer.

I replaced the transmitter to its hook. "Breakups," I said to Bjørn with a shrug.

He glanced my way but didn't acknowledge my comment.

I chewed my thumbnail, trying to figure out what to do next. With Dalton backing off, I was on my own. The remote cam had better work. My best strategy now was to lie low, give Ray no reason to even think of me again. I'd wait until I was sure I had incriminating video before I made my move. That's when I'd…I wasn't sure yet. I'd figure something out.

"Did you love him?"

"What?" I turned in surprise. Bjørn initiating conversation was so unexpected.

He gestured aft with his head, referring to the following boat. "I saw you two in the pub. I don't know what happened between you—" he turned to face me "—but that boy loves you."

My mouth opened, but I didn't know what to say.

He grinned. "I might be an old codger, but I recognize love when I see it. He had that look in his eyes."

"He and I, we…" I shook my head.

Bjørn smirked. "Young 'uns. Can't tell 'em nothing."

The door swept open. Michael came barreling in, his finger pointing forward. "Orca! Off the starboard bow!"

Bjørn calmly swung forward, raised a pair of binoculars, and nodded. His shoulders sagged with resignation.

Michael, on the other hand, was fired up like a kid waiting to rip his Christmas stocking down from the hearth. I followed him out to the rail. Five hundred yards or more in the distance, a pod of killer whales moved through the waves, their distinctive triangular dorsal fins breaking the surface. Unlike the slow, steady movement of the humpback whales, these predators cut through the water with menacing speed.

There were at least twenty of them.

Bjørn throttled up the engine and changed course. Right for the whales.

"You stay inside, in the galley or down below," Michael said and turned to join his father.

"What? I want to see the whales."

He spun around and grabbed me by the arm. "You do as I say. Do you understand?"

Every fiber of my being wanted to smack that stern, I'm-in-charge look off his face. "Fine," I managed in a wimpy voice.

He stormed off. This was it. They were going to try to capture one.

I had to let Dalton know. My phone read no service. *Damn. Damn. Dammit!*

The radio. But Bjørn was in there at the helm. What could I say? What excuse could I give?

I'd think of something. I went back into the pilothouse and straight to the radio.

"Don't touch that," Bjørn said, his voice calm.

"I forgot to mention—"

"Doesn't matter. Ray's using it now with the handheld."

The radio had been switched to a working channel. Ray's voice came over the line. "Flank from the east."

"Yes, sir," a voice crackled back.

I had to come up with a reason to stay in the wheelhouse so I'd know what was going on. I looked at Bjørn and he looked at me and frowned. He wasn't happy about something.

"Coffee?" I suggested with a casual smile.

He studied my face for a long moment before responding with a nod.

"I'll get some brewing," I said and slipped out the door.

Dylan wasn't in the galley. Probably on deck, helping get ready for the capture. I filled the pot with water and ground coffee and set it on the stove to percolate.

Then I paced, my stomach churning up a sour bile that fumed at the back of my throat. How was I supposed to stand by and wait while they were about to do…what they were about to do?

I checked my phone again. Still no service. *Dalton, please turn back.* If my remote camera didn't work, all this was for nothing. And even if it did, I had no way of uploading the footage right away. If I was made, the digital files would be here on the boat with me. Ray could easily destroy them—and me—and get away with it.

I paced some more, twirling the bracelet my dad had given me, round and round my wrist. How was I going to hide my feelings and pretend this was no big deal? Then how long would I be stuck on this boat with them before I had a chance to escape?

Maybe I could mutiny. Dylan would most likely be an ally. And Bjørn, well, I was sure he wasn't too keen on this. Maybe he wouldn't help, but wouldn't interfere either? That left me against Ray and Michael.

The boat slowed. The engine quieted. I crawled across the bench and looked out the window. The pod of orcas was directly alongside. This was happening.

My dad always told me, where there's a will, there's a way. When your heart's in the right place.

I gave my bracelet another twist. *Oh Daddy, you died with your heart in the right place.*

But I can't stand by and do nothing.

CHAPTER 18

I dumped the entire pot of coffee into a Thermos and hustled back up the stairs to the wheelhouse. Bjørn was standing at the door, looking out the window, his arms crossed.

"Hot coffee," I said, pushing past him and reaching for his cup.

He nodded without comment.

"Bjørn, what's going on?" I said as I poured.

He accepted the cup from me and took a sip. He acted like he was savoring it before he answered, but then his eyes turned misty. "Best if you don't know."

"Why? What do you mean?"

"Little lady, you should've stayed with that other boy. This one's up to no good."

"What are you talking about? What's going on?"

He took another sip of the coffee. "Like I said—"

"It's better I don't know. Yeah, I got it." I was disappointed. I hoped he'd tell me now. I needed to know for sure if he was an ally. "Mind if I stay in here with you?"

Ray came busting through the door. His eyes settled on me and his lip curved into a snarl. "What did I tell you?" he said as he went straight for the deck controls. "Out!"

"I was just—"

"Leave her be. She brought me coffee," Bjørn said.

Ray flicked a switch, fiddled with a joystick, and the whirring of the winch rattled the floorboards. They were deploying the seine nets. Michael and Dylan were on deck, hauling the nets and making sure they went into the water without getting tangled.

I made like a chameleon and blended in with the paneling.

Bjørn eased the engine throttle forward, turned the wheel, and steered the boat in a circle as the nets unfurled into the ocean.

Bjørn gestured out the front windows. "Svein and Jænis are here."

Two small speedboats zig-zagged through the waves beyond the whales, criss-crossing each other in an irregular pattern, heading toward us. They zoomed back and forth, herding the whales, making them disoriented and scaring them into changing direction, driving them toward the nets.

I watched with my fingernails dug into my palms, an expression of innocent curiosity pasted on my face.

Bjørn had steered more than a half circle and was closing the loop. The pod was now a few hundred yards off the starboard bow, the whales crowded into a confused bunch.

"Gotcha," said Ray. He pulled back the winch control stick, locked it into place and pushed through the door, heading back out on deck.

Out of nowhere, a small prop plane dropped from above and buzzed along the surface of the water, right toward the whales.

I stepped out on the deck as it roared over my head.

The whales dove and surfaced in frantic patterns, running into each other, their formation getting tighter as they called out with their distinctive chitters and squeaks. I shook with anger. I had to stop this right now before—*no, it'll be okay. Get the video you came for first.*

A few whales slipped from the main pod, but the boats let them go now, staying on the core group, forcing them forward, toward the nets. Ray was taking advantage of the killer whales' strong family instinct. The pod would remain tightly bunched together for support, making them easy to corral into the net.

The orcas dove and changed direction as though they recognized the nets and were looking for an open gap to escape.

I clenched and unclenched my fists. *Damn you, Ray Goldman. You're going to rot in prison for this.*

Then the whales dove, as though synchronized, and disappeared. Ray came charging back up the stairs. "Which way did they go?"

Bjørn shrugged with indifference.

About five males surfaced with a loud whoosh. "There!" Ray shouted into the radio. "Flank 'em. Flank 'em."

Both speedboats zoomed toward the whales and cut them off, making them turn back toward the nets.

Then came another whoosh. The other whales—the females and younger ones—surfaced past the nets. They'd slipped around.

"Dammit!" Ray slammed his fist down on the console. He glared at Bjørn as if it were all his fault. "Michael, get those nets back in," he spat into the handheld radio, then slammed the joystick forward and the winch squealed into motion. "I'm too old for this," he grumbled.

I suppressed a grin. They'd worked together and outsmarted him. *Ha! Way to go whales!*

Bringing in the nets took several minutes and the orcas were getting away.

Ray shouted some indiscernible command on the radio and the speedboats chased them down. The plane circled back, flying low over the water, and the whales dove in fear.

"Damn lines are jammin' it." Ray slammed the winch joystick back. "Don't you dare let them get away, boys. Force them back," he barked into the radio as he pushed through the door, then bounded down the stairs, shouting at Michael.

I held the door open behind him, watching through the

opening.

One of the speedboats turned and zoomed along the far side of the pod. The driver raised a gun and fired something into the water. Two seconds later, an explosion reverberated across the water. The whales surfaced in a panic, blowing with frightful force, squealing and screeching.

I rushed back into the wheelhouse, slamming the door behind me. I stared down Bjørn. "What are they doing?" I knew. They were using seal bombs, explosive devices similar to M-80 firecrackers, to scare and disorient the whales. But I wanted him to say it.

Another bomb was fired into the water. Kaboom! Then another. Kaboom! The whales became frantic, churning up the water in their terror. The boats circled around them, forcing them into a bunch.

"Get this old tug in gear," Ray ordered Bjørn over the radio.

"Yessir," Bjørn said, but he took his time getting to the throttle.

Dylan pushed through the door and came to a halt, his eyes on Bjørn. "Yer man towl me ter run de winch." His hands shook and he looked as if he expected to be drawn and quartered if he didn't get to it right now.

Bjørn shrugged, so Dylan lunged toward the console and fired it up, his hands fumbling at the controls. The nets once again unfurled into the sea.

More seal bombs went off. Kaboom! Kaboom!

Ray's voice thundered over the radio, shouting orders as Bjørn pulled back on the throttle. The nets were fully deployed. The speedboats closed in, pushing the frantic whales inside.

My guts churned, building an unbearable pressure in my belly. I took hold of the edge of the console, trying to steady myself for fear I'd burst like a water balloon.

Ray would adjust the nets now, cinching up the bottom, then the top, forcing the whales closer and closer together, making it easy to get one lassoed. I kept my vigil. Once he had the nets cinched and the whales next to the boat, that was my cue to start the camera recording. My blood pumped double-time in my veins.

Bjørn set the boat to idle, took a sip of his coffee, then leaned back on the console and crossed his arms. "I've got it now," he said to Dylan, dismissing him. As soon as Dylan was out the door, he turned to me. "I'd go down below, I were you," he said, barely above a whisper. "Before he comes back."

I nodded to Bjørn. Staying clear of Ray was a good idea. I couldn't risk him seeing me start the camera with the remote. Or that I'd lose it and beat him to a bloody pulp before I had my evidence.

Having the whales in the nets definitely constituted harassment. Hell, the seal bombs alone were enough to arrest him, but once he had a whale in the sling, there was no denying his intent. That was what I needed on video to nail him to the wall. That was the moment I'd confront him. Stop this terror. I'd bluff, tell him I'd instantly uploaded a video via satellite link. It was plausible enough. A good plan.

You're going down, Ray Goldman.

I slipped out the door and headed for the galley where I'd be able to see the progress as they pulled in the nets.

The orcas swam round and round inside the net, checking out the boundaries, their exhalations faster and more rapid, sending spurts of misty-spray into the air with loud, forceful breaths. It sounded like they were hyperventilating. Some spy-hopped, vertically pushing themselves out of the water like a human treading water, trying to see. Others slapped their flukes and flippers on the surface of the water, a rapid-fire thwack-thwack-thwack while vocalizing with their high-pitched calls.

The few whales that had not been forced into the nets were now circling outside it, frantically calling out to those trapped inside. Their shrill cries turned my insides out.

The winch fired up again, clankety-clanking as it slowly

pulled in the net, drawing the circle in tighter and tighter. Inside the circle, there were twelve whales in all—eight adults, three juveniles, and staying next to her mother, an infant. Baby Kimmy.

My lip began to quiver. *Don't think about it, McVie.*

I checked my phone again. Still no service. *C'mon, Dalton. I need you.* I pushed the button on the remote, starting my video recording, and sent a silent prayer to the Valkyries for support. Vengeance and retribution were in order. *Vengeance and retribution.*

The winch shuddered and stopped. The whales were now confined inside a net that had been cinched down around them to an area the size of a small swimming pool. The whales became docile, lying at the surface along the line of floats, facing out to sea, their voices now reduced to a low moaning-like hum. It was as though they were already giving up.

Ray reached into one of the lazarettes, extracting an aluminum pole with a noose on the end, then extended it to its full length, and headed for the aft deck. I slipped out the galley door and moved to where I could see.

Michael was there, pointing. Ray came alongside him, pole in hand. He lowered it into the water, adjusting the noose, and as Michael pointed, Ray worked the lasso.

Soon, they'd be raising one in the harness. The act I was waiting for. Not long now. I couldn't watch, but I had to watch. I glanced up at the crow's nest. Too far away to see the camera, to confirm that the little red light was on.

Ray had already made a choice from the group and was trying to get it lassoed. They'd pick the healthiest, most robust one, a teenager, young enough to train, old enough to be strong and healthy for the long journey and the time it took for training, not to mention the transition to living in captivity.

I kept my distance, waiting for my moment.

Then Ray dropped to his knees. He had one lassoed around the neck. He let out a whoop. I stepped forward, trying to get a look. He had ahold of the lasso, towing a whale to the side of the boat. I took another step to see and stopped cold.

The baby. He had captured the baby.

Noooooo! Not baby Kimmy! The tiny whale twisted and twirled against the noose while her mother thrashed in the water next to her. I spun around, my eyes stinging, my throat contracting. *Don't let them see you.* I pressed my fingers underneath my cheekbones trying to hold back the tears.

What in the world was Ray thinking? He had to know she was still nursing. How on earth did he plan to keep her alive? Why take the risk? This didn't make sense. None of it. Dr. Parker had said they would take an older whale, an adolescent that was more likely to survive and—

Then it hit me. Ocean World of Miami. They'd been advertising for months, anticipating a captive-born baby whale. News outlets had been picking up the story, splashing headlines across the nation's papers.

All zoos and aquariums rely on signature species—cute and cuddly panda bears, big cats, gorillas—as their main attractions. The only attraction that brought more attention was a new baby, of any species. And with a baby orca, they had the best of both. A marketer's dream. Ocean World was planning special celebration days at the park, with parades and fireworks. They'd already sold out tickets. Baby orca dolls were flying off the shelves.

Had something happened to the infant? Dr. Parker had said an unnatural percentage of captive-bred babies are stillborn. Had it already happened? If the press got wind of it, they'd have a heyday. Ocean World would lose millions. Were they planning to slip a wild-caught baby into its place, hoping the mother would adopt it as her own and no one would be the wiser?

No wonder Ray hadn't bothered with a larger boat. Baby Kimmy had been the golden prize all along.

It took everything in my power to keep my feet planted

where they were. Even my hair hurt from containing my fury.

Ray and Michael yanked and pulled, dragging the infant to the side of the boat while the mother thrashed beside her, flipping her tail, churning up the water around them, all the while calling with agonizing squeals of anguish.

How they were immune to her torment was beyond my comprehension. My heart was damn near ripped from my chest.

You've got a mouth full of teeth. Now's the time to use them!

Michael lowered the sling into the water and got it under the baby, slid her tiny pectoral fins into the slits made for that purpose, then gave a thumbs up to Bjørn in the wheelhouse.

My fury threatened to consume my soul. *Ten more seconds, McVie.* The winch creaked into action and as the baby was lifted from the water, the entire pod of whales became silent. As if being taken from the water meant certain death, they gave up.

CHAPTER 19

It was now or never. I'd either gotten the video or not. I charged down the deck, shouting, "Put her back in the water! She's just a baby! Put her back in the water!"

Michael looked up at me. His eyes narrowed. "I told you to stay inside."

The baby whale's little snout was the only part I could see, poking out from the canvas sling. The mother now floated motionless in the sea.

I swallowed hard. "Put her back into the water right now and—"

"Dammit!" Ray was on his feet and charging toward me. "What the hell did I tell you about him?" he bellowed as he brushed past me.

What? I spun around. Behind us, the *Sea Mist* bobbed in the sea. *Dalton!* I'd been too distracted to notice. *Yes!*

Ray flung open the lid of a lazarette, grabbed the rocket-propelled grenade launcher, raised it to his shoulder, and aimed.

No! I pounced on his back just as he pulled the trigger. He slammed into the lazarette, doubling over the edge. The grenade rocketed toward its target and hit the *Sea Mist* in her bow, shattering it to pieces in a fiery explosion.

My heart stopped. I couldn't breathe. *No, no, no, no! Dalton! No!* A ball of fire hovered over the water.

Ray regained his balance and tossed the grenade launcher into its case. He spun on me. "You bitch!"

I dropped my head and lunged, pinning him against the side of the lazarette.

"Knock it off!"

Ray smirked.

I pulled back and spun around.

Michael held a revolver pointed at me. "You're not going to make any more trouble, now, are you?" he spat, his eyes ablaze.

My eyes traveled from Michael's face to the weapon in his hand, where I fixated. A Smith & Wesson J-Frame, the most popular revolver on the market. Accurate. Deadly. His hand held it steady.

What the hell had I been thinking? *Dalton. Dead. And*—I shook my head, my lip quivering, tears stinging at the back of my eyes. *I'm way over my head.*

"You wanted a job," Michael sneered. "Keep that fish alive. Or when I toss its rotting carcass overboard, you'll go with it. Got it?"

I stared back at him and managed to nod. Beyond him, a pillar of black smoke billowed skyward from the *Sea Mist*, but she was still afloat. Flames engulfed the bow. I conjured a silent prayer for Dalton. There was a chance. Maybe he'd seen it coming. He could be okay. And Dr. Parker…

I had to keep calm, do my job.

Breathe in. Breathe out.

"I suggest you forget your boyfriend and get to work," Ray growled.

"Yes, sir," I said. I turned to Dylan, who stood stone still, gripping the end of a net line, white-faced, his mouth hinged open. "Will you please help me get her into the hold. We need to keep her wet and her temperature down."

Dylan snapped out of his daze and immediately started following my commands.

Ray shouted up to Bjørn in the wheelhouse and the winch creaked into service. As the baby whale was lowered into the shallow water in the bottom of the holding tank and started to float, Dylan and I tried to unhook the sling from the cable.

"'Tis stuck," Dylan said.

I got up on the rim of the tank and tried to work the hook from the harness. It was wedged in too tightly.

"What's the problem?" said Michael.

"It's stuck," I said.

He shoved me to the side. "I'll get it." He halted, glared at me. "You must think I'm stupid."

"What?" I had no idea what he meant.

He turned to Ray and handed him the gun. "Keep it pointed at her," he said.

Michael took the hook from me and, with sheer might, worked it free. At least he could see I wasn't lying.

With a grunt, he stepped down from the edge of the tank, wiped his hands on the front of his pants, and without a word, he and Ray went to work pulling in the net. They were letting the other whales go.

I stared at the baby, my hands interlaced over the top of my head. I was supposed to keep her alive. My insides burned with rage. *I'm not a real vet!* What had Dr. Parker said, to keep it cool, the areas that are vascularized? What had I been thinking? I looked at Dylan for help. He was staring at me, wide-eyed, waiting for me to tell him what to do.

I turned around and stared at the *Sea Mist*, worry threatening to shut me down. *No. Dalton can take care of himself.* He'd been trained by the best in the world. He knew exactly what to do.

If he wasn't dead.

The flames had died down, but black smoke still wafted from the *Sea Mist*. Debris floated in the water around the main hull, which was still partially afloat. It was too far for me to see anyone on board. *Dammit, Dalton. I told you to stay back.*

Dylan touched me on the shoulder. "What's wrong wi' it?"

I spun back around. The baby orca was listing to the side, her eyes closed. She floated, but made no movement, no attempt to stay upright.

"Tighten the sling back up a little," I said taking hold of the roping on my side and tying it off. "Just enough to keep her upright and her blowhole out of the water."

"It doesn't luk loike she's breathin'." Dylan's face was pasty white. He'd stared down the barrel of Michael's revolver, too.

Baby Kimmy's tongue lolled out of the side of her mouth.

"She's in shock," I said, trying my damnedest to sound like I knew what I was talking about. Not that I knew what the hell to do about it.

"The water in the tank is too warm. Buckets of sea water," I said to Dylan. "Pour them over her."

He stared, nodding like a bobble-head.

"You got a bucket?" I said.

"Oh yeah," he said and turned a full circle before finding direction.

I held my hand a few inches over her blowhole. Nothing. I couldn't feel the slightest bit of air.

I closed my eyes. *Please breathe. Breathe! C'mon. You can do it.*

Dylan was back, slowly dumping water over her back.

"On her fins," I said. "Her flippers and her tail."

The winch stopped. The net was back on board. The engines fired up again and the boat lurched into gear.

Ray came up behind me. "What's going on?"

"She's uh…nothing. Everything's fine."

He turned to poor Dylan who looked like he'd wet his pants. "She's not breathin'," he blurted out.

Ray spun on me. "Well, get it breathing."

I stared at him, wishing for a fillet knife. I'd have happily demonstrated the workings of the mammalian lungs as I eviscerated him.

Michael came up behind him. "You're a vet, ain't ya?"

"Yeah, but—"

"It's simple, chicky," said Ray, pulling the revolver from his pocket and shoving it at me. "It lives, you live. It dies…" He held up his free hand and shrugged.

This amazing calm came over me. All my anger and fury simply disappeared. I was going to die either way. Once they sold baby Kimmy, passed her into someone else's care, I'd be a liability. A witness to the crime. No matter whether they ever knew I was an agent or not.

My fate was in my own hands.

I sized Ray up. With a quick lunge, I could take him down. But what would Michael do? I wasn't sure I could handle them both. But now Ray had the weapon. An advantage to me. He was the easier of the two to take down.

Dylan wouldn't fight me. But would he help? I wasn't sure. I had to wait for the chance to take them by surprise, one at a time.

Right now, my priority was to get this baby breathing. There was nothing I could do to help Dalton. My stomach clenched. He was on his own too. *Oh Dalton.*

The baby whale floated in the sling. No sign of life. It was a mammal. I could try CPR. Dogs have been saved by CPR. But how would I do it? How do I blow into that mouth? Could I blow into the hole?

I rested my hand on the baby's back, trying to feel a breath. Nothing.

"I'm not sure—" I started to shake, all the feelings returning in a rush. The sharp prickle of tears threatened behind my eyelids. I blinked them back. My chest tightened and I struggled for air. I stepped back, closed my eyes, and drew in a long breath. "I'm not sure I can."

Ray took the radio from his belt. "Bjørn," he said. "Call the men back. I'm not going home empty-handed."

CHAPTER 20

The boat changed direction. The high-pitched hum of the speedboats echoed in the distance. They'd drop more bombs in the water. They'd push the whales back into the nets. This was happening. Again.

Something inside me snapped. I'd be damned if he was going to kill another whale. I needed to stop this insanity and get to Dalton. But how? *Think!*

Ray headed for the bridge to run the winch. Michael turned to work the nets.

I looked up and down the length of the winch. It was the key. If I could disable it, he'd have nothing. "Stay with her," I said to Dylan. "Keep her wet."

"But oi tart yer said—"

"Just do it, okay." I didn't need Dylan giving me away.

I sneaked around the backside of the winch, hiding from Michael's view. As the net was drawn in, the winch turned, wrapping a cable around the drum. To let out the net, the drums turned in the opposite direction, unfurling the cable. If I could shove something in there as the nets were being deployed again, maybe I'd foul it. But what? I looked around the deck. What was strong enough, but couldn't be easily yanked back out? Something that would bind it up for good?

I crossed the deck as we bounced through the waves. There must be something in one of the lazarettes. The extra floats maybe. If one got crushed in the drum, would it cause enough damage to make it inoperable? I sorted through the pile, trying to find anything.

The engine idled down. The winch started to turn. Michael had his back to me, guiding the nets into the water.

The wheelhouse door slammed and Ray came down the stairs toward me, his eyes on Michael and the nets. This was my chance. As he rushed by, I swiped his ankle with my foot. He stumbled forward, trying to catch his balance, and I pounced on his back, slamming him to the deck.

He rolled, wrenching his arm free, and grabbed me by the hair. Nothing pisses me off more than being grabbed by the hair. I brought up my knee and rammed him right in the crotch. He bent inward with a groan. "Bitch!" he managed.

I got to my knees, reached around and grabbed his ass, right on his duct-taped wound.

He howled in pain.

"This *bitch* is a trained federal agent," I said and brought my elbow down on his neck, knocking him out cold. I reached into his pocket and spun around, the revolver sighted on Michael. He still had his back to me, concentrating on his job.

I let out my breath.

Dylan peeked around the winch, his eyes wide.

"Help me tie him up," I said to Dylan, making sure I didn't take my eyes off Michael. "Grab that old piece of net. And that line."

Dylan obeyed, scurrying about like a puppy bringing me toys.

Once Dylan had Ray's hands tied, I moved to the back of the boat, to Michael. "Drop what you're doing and put your hands up where I can see them."

He looked over his shoulder at me and froze with his mouth open. So he hadn't suspected me of being an agent. His eyes flicked to Ray, then back to me, his expression turning from surprise to anger.

"I'm a federal officer," I said. "He's under arrest. And so are you. Put your hands where I can see them."

Michael looked to his father, then back to me. "Do you seriously think—"

"Your hands!"

He slowly raised his hands, but I got the sense it was to placate me, not a gesture of surrender. His lip curled up into a plastic smile. "It was only this one. Just one. To get back on our feet."

"And you have the right to remain silent," I said. "So do it." I didn't care what he had to say, the arrogant, lying son of a bitch. "Get over there and sit down," I told him, gesturing toward Ray. I gave Dylan an encouraging nod. "Tie him up, too."

With his narrowed eyes glued on me and the gun, Michael edged toward his father, but there was something about the way he moved, the way he carefully placed each footstep.

"Get down on the deck. Now," I said.

He stopped, eyeing me with disdain. "You gonna make me?" His voice had lowered an octave, the boyish charm vanished. "You think I'm an idiot? You got no authority to arrest me or my dad. This is a foreign country." Without taking his eyes from me, he said, "Dylan, untie him."

Poor Dylan. The boy bit down hard on his lip, his eyes flicking back and forth from me to Michael.

"She's not going to hurt you, Dylan," Michael said, his words dripping with hostility.

Dylan remained where he stood, frozen in place while I debated what the hell to do.

"Dammit, Dylan!" Michael shouted

Dylan lurched back with a start.

"What the hell?" It was Ray, coming to. He blinked a couple times, his eyes working to focus.

"Fine, I'll do it," Michael said to Dylan and turned toward his father.

I fired. The gunshot echoed across the water.

Michael jerked upright, surprise and uncertainty in his expression.

"Are you resisting arrest?" I said, aiming the weapon at his chest. "Because if you are, I've got just cause to shoot."

"Michael, sit down," said Ray. "She's all fluff. She's got nothing. It don't matter if she's an agent. It's still her word against ours."

Michael stared at his father, unsure.

"That fish was dead when we pulled it out of the water. We was just curious, was all. Ain't nobody gonna tell the difference." He was nodding, urging Michael to understand. "So just sit down and don't go making it worse."

Atta boy. Good old Ray.

Michael stared at me as if trying to decide whether to charge me, see if I'd follow through on my threat to shoot. Finally, he slumped to the floor beside his father, a scowl on his face. Dylan hurried to tie him up.

I checked both their wrists and told Dylan to also tie their ankles before I bounded up the stairs to the pilothouse.

Dalton and April were probably in the water by now, hypothermic—if they were still alive. I crashed through the doorway, the weapon held in front of me. "Turn this boat around," I demanded. "We need to go get them. Turn this boat around."

The two speedboats were circling the orcas. The airplane was back, flying low toward us. "Do it now!"

Bjørn held up one hand in surrender as he reached for the microphone for the radio with the other and shouted orders in Norwegian. The only word I recognized was Svein. One of the speedboats changed its course and headed for the *Sea Mist*. Bjørn turned to me. "He can get there much faster."

I motioned with the gun. "Still, turn this boat around, too."

"I can't. The nets are in the water."

I pointed at the winch controls. "Then get 'em back on

board."

Bjørn shook his head. "We can't without a man on deck. If the nets get tangled, we'd have to cut them loose."

"Fine," I said. "Dylan will do it."

"Svein'll have them in the boat before we could move. Don't worry."

My training would have me subdue Bjørn right now too, to be sure to neutralize any threat, but he was a Norwegian citizen. And he was cooperating. And my gut told me I could trust him. Right now, I needed him to stop this nightmare.

"Just the same," I said. "Get 'em in."

I hollered down the stairs for Dylan to bring in the nets. Bjørn worked the controls while the winch tick-tick-ticked. I swear I could've hauled them in faster by hand.

I found the binoculars. All I could do was watch out the back window, powerless to help Dalton. The speedboat slowed alongside a floating piece, what remained of the hull. Then something was hauled into the boat, but on the far side. I couldn't see anything. Then a figure stood up. It was April.

The boat was put into gear again, circling. *Dalton's there, too. He's got to be there. Somewhere.* My hands shook.

Then the boat slowed again and they were reaching for something. *Please let it be Dalton. Please.*

The crew of two hauled something up over the side. A man? Was it Dalton?

A seal bomb exploded in the water in front of the *Forseti*. I spun around. The whales flipped and turned in a panicked frenzy. *Dammit!* "Stop that right now!"

Bjørn held up his hand. "All right." He went to the radio.

I went back out on deck, tucked the weapon in the back of my jeans, and headed for the stern. The speedboat was pulling up alongside our vessel. I raced to the side. Besides the driver, two figures were on board, wool blankets wrapped around their shoulders. Dalton threw off the blanket and rose to toss a line to Dylan. My legs went weak. He was alive. *Alive!* I gripped the side of the boat, my whole body shaking with relief.

"Are you all right?" I shouted over the engine.

Dalton nodded. April looked shaken, but she was alive. Wet strands of hair stuck to the side of her face, her lips drained of color. Dylan helped her onto the *Forseti*.

"He saved my life," she said, shivering. "I've never seen anything like it. He was calm as could be."

Dalton stepped aboard behind her. I barreled into him, my arms wrapped around his shoulders. "You're all right," I cried. "You're all right." I squeezed until I was sure he was real.

"I don't know what I would have done," April said, gazing at him as if he wore a cape and tights. "Suddenly, out of nowhere, kaboom, and the whole boat was on fire. It was…" She shook. "Dalton got it contained with the extinguishers, but then"—she squeezed her eyes shut—"the cabin starting filling with water."

"She's in shock, but I kept her out of the water until our rescue boat came," Dalton said, all business. "We got splashed then, but briefly. What happened here?"

Svein, the driver, was right behind Dalton. The informant. "Yeah, what's going on?" he asked.

I shook the man's hand. "Thank you for saving them, Svein."

He hesitated and I got the idea he didn't like that I knew his name. His buggy eyes darted about, looking for Ray, I assumed.

"It's all right." I gestured toward the men who were leaning against the bulkhead, their hands tied behind their backs. "They're in custody now. We owe you our thanks." *And I'm sorry I called you Potato Head.*

"Are you all right?" Dalton asked me.

"Yeah," I said with a reassuring smile. "After Ray fired on you, Michael pulled a weapon on me. But I subdued them."

He raised one eyebrow. "Subdued?"

I gave him a what-can-I-say shrug.

"Don't say nothing," Ray shouted to Svein.

Svein looked to me, then back toward Ray. "You're arresting them, then?" He moved toward Ray.

I followed, talking to his backside. "Yes, we have the evidence we need."

He stood with his arms crossed, looking down at Ray. "So he won't be coming back here? He's going to prison?"

"Yep."

"She's lying," Ray spat. "She's got nothing."

"Not true." I pointed to the crow's nest. "I've got video of the whole thing."

His eyes traveled to the crow's nest and back.

"It don't matter. You came under false pretenses."

"Bong. Wrong again," I said. "You invited me on board. And I am not required to identify myself as an agent thanks to Hoffa v. United States, 1966. Oh, and the videotape, that's admissible thanks to U.S. v. Wahchumwah, 2012."

Ray had his lips clamped together so tight I thought his head might blow off.

"You lying bitch!" Michael said and leapt to his feet and charged me. Somehow, he'd gotten his hands untied. He plowed into to me, knocking me off my feet. We slammed to the deck. Blew the wind right out of me. Then Dalton was there, lifting Michael off of me, Michael's arms flailing at him. It all happened so fast.

"I took you once, I'll do it again," Michael threatened him, his face red.

Dalton smirked. He looked to me as I got to my feet. "He needs a serious attitude adjustment."

"Well," I said, brushing myself off. "I think you deserve the honors."

Dalton shook his head. "Wouldn't be a fair contest."

"No, really," I said. "You took the fall and all."

"Both of you can shut up," said Michael, raising the gun and pointing it at me.

My hand went to my waistband. *Crap!*

Dalton lunged, knocking the gun from Michael's hand and slamming him to the floor. In an instant, Dalton had him pinned, bent over and moaning, his elbow twisted into an arm lock.

Svein picked up the gun.

"Nice move," I said to Dalton, shaking.

"Now apologize to the lady," Dalton said.

"Screw you," Michael spat.

Dalton twisted harder. "Nobody talks to Poppy like that."

Michael's face flushed red.

"Apologize"—he twisted harder—"or I'll demonstrate my—"

"I'm sorry. I'm sorry," he groaned.

Dalton let up and Dylan scurried forward, the rope in his hand.

Dalton tied Michael back up and shoved him to the floor. "Now stay," he said.

I took a quick glance around. April's eyes were wide, her mouth hanging open.

Svein looked annoyed more than anything. He stepped toward the fish hold. "What about the whale?"

"I…" My eyes met Dalton's. "I couldn't save her."

Dalton gazed back at me, his eyes filled with sympathy. I wanted to fall into his arms and cry my eyes out.

"What are you saying?" Svein said, holding me back from making a fool of myself.

"The capture was too traumatic. She didn't make it."

April pushed past me, rushing to the tank where the baby whale floated, motionless.

Dalton followed.

"There was nothing I could do," I said, my tongue stuck in my throat.

The airplane buzzed low overhead, blowing my hair around and into my face. "I told him to call them off!"

"I'm on it," Dylan volunteered and took the stairs two at a time.

The pod of whales appeared off the starboard side, emitting squeaky calls in their panic. We all rushed to the side of the boat. One of the killer whales surfaced and let out a wail like I'd never heard.

"That's K-12," April said. "The mother. That's the calf's mother."

From behind us came a tiny squeal in response. The baby. My eyes met Dalton's. "She's alive!"

CHAPTER 21

I spun around and raced back to the tank. "She's alive! She's alive!" Dylan, flying back down the stairs, grinned ear to ear and wrapped his arms around me.

"We need to get her back in the water," I said. "Get the winch cable. Get the winch cable!"

Dylan leaped into action.

I grabbed hold of the edge of the sling to hook it to the cable. "Dalton, help me with this."

April was there, taking hold of the other side.

I couldn't believe it. *She's alive!*

"Not so fast."

I whipped around.

Svein held the gun pointed at me. "Back off."

"What?" I shook my head in disbelief. "No. We need to get her back in the water."

"She's not going anywhere." He pointed the gun at Dalton, then back to me. "That's a million dollar whale, right there. Now step back."

I slowly lifted my hands into the air. "I don't understand. You're the one who called us here. You're the informant." *How did I not see that coming? I let him pick up the gun. He should just take my badge, too.*

"What's going on?" Bjørn hollered. He was coming down the stairs from the wheelhouse.

"Mind your business, old man," Svein called to him over his shoulder, his eyes on me and Dalton.

Dalton took a step away from me. Then another step. He was trying to cause Svein to split his attention, put him at a greater disadvantage.

"Americans. The world's policemen. Always sticking your noses where they don't belong. There was no doubt you'd come." He smirked and his cheeks puffed out like a baked potato. I wanted to poke him right in the eye with a fork. "Now do your job. Take those two thieves back to America." He gestured toward the speedboat. "Take them and go."

Dalton took another step. He was weighing the odds. If we were far enough apart and Svein fired the weapon, one or the other of us had a chance to take him down before he could turn and fire a second round.

"We're not going anywhere," I said, trying to keep his attention on me and away from Dalton.

Baby Kimmy wiggled and squealed for her mother.

"And you're not taking this whale."

Dalton shook his head. Subtle, but I saw it. He didn't want me to provoke Svein. Just keep his attention. But I meant it, dammit. I wasn't going anywhere until she was back in the water with her mother.

"You have no authority here," Svein said. "In fact, I'm quite sure you were told to go home, that you aren't welcome by the Norwegian government."

"How'd you know about that?"

He took a step forward, an amused grin on his spud face. "This is my land. My sea."

"That was your plan all along," I said. "Let Ray do the dirty work, then take the fall, while you took off with the whale and cashed in."

"I knew you were sharp." He winked his buggy, potato eye. "You go on home and throw them in jail and smile pretty when you get your award. The rest is none of your business." He turned toward Dalton and raised the gun in warning. "Don't make the mistake of underestimating me. Now step back."

Dalton did as he commanded, his hands in the air.

Thwack! Svein slumped to the floor. Bjørn stood behind him, a fire extinguisher in his hands, his eyes on the baby whale. "This isn't right," he said, shaking his head. "This isn't right."

Dalton and I pounced on Svein. Dylan was there with some rope to tie his hands.

Bjørn set down the extinguisher. "No respect. Men like him…" His eyes traveled to Ray. "And men like him. No respect."

Dalton took the rope from Dylan with a quick thanks and wrapped it around Svein's wrists.

I took Dylan by the arm. "Get that winch going."

"Roi on," he said.

April, Dalton, and I held up the sides of the sling while Bjørn clamped on the hook.

"Lift her up," he hollered up to Dylan in the wheelhouse.

The winch clanked into gear, the cable pulled taut, and it started to lift, then—snap! One of the ropes broke. Then—snap!—another.

"Down! Bring her back down!" Bjørn shouted.

The winch creaked to a halt.

"Dammit!" I looked at Dalton, anger burning in my belly. "I cut the ropes. I tried to ruin the harness, but Michael caught me. I didn't get it finished."

"Well, let's see what we can do to fix it," he said, his voice calm.

The baby squealed. The whales in the water squeaked and called back.

"That's a support call," said April. "I think they know we're trying to help."

"We need to hurry," I said.

Bjørn pointed to a bin. "The tool chest is there. Extra lines and net over here." He rushed to a lazarette.

While we went to work, April poured buckets of sea water on the orca baby, trying to keep her cool.

"This isn't going to work," Bjørn said, tangles of net in his hands.

"It has to," I said.

"There's plenty of net," said Dalton. "We can get something rigged pretty easily to hold her. But how do we make sure she can get out once we've lowered her into the water? What if she gets tangled in it?"

"Get it rigged. I'll worry about that," I said.

Bjørn and Dalton cut lengths of rope and net and we shoved it under the baby whale and secured it to the harness while she chirped to her mother.

"That should hold," Bjørn said. "But—"

"I got it," I said.

Dylan put the winch into motion and I crawled up the side of the holding tank, placed my feet on either side of the harness, and grabbed on tightly to the cable. I held out my hand to Dalton. "Give me your KA-BAR."

"Are you serious? That's your plan?"

"Gimme the knife!"

He shook his head, a frown on his face. "You don't know what those adult whales out there will do."

"You're right. I don't know."

"I'm telling you," said April. "They know we're trying to help."

"Yeah," Dalton turned on her. "What if you're wrong? We can't risk it."

"I'm not wrong." She held his gaze.

"Dalton, gimme the knife!"

His eyes flicked from her to me. "This is insane," he said as he pulled the knife from its sheath on his belt and handed it to me.

The winch arm turned and the whale and I swung sideways.

Bjørn hollered. "You should have a life jacket on."

"No time!"

Dalton watched, shaking his head, his hands on his hips.

We hung there, suspended over the water. The baby chittered away, her voice getting higher in pitch. The adult whales circled, popping up to get a look at us, slapping fins and calling with a haunting fervor.

The winch shuttered and clanked and the cable started to lower us.

As soon as we were a few feet from the surface, I began to saw at the net with the knife.

Killer whales circled, closer and closer. Heads popped up and submerged again, circling. Five, six, maybe more. I sawed and sawed.

One surfaced right next to us and splashed. The frigid water hit me in the face and soaked my hair. It took my breath away. I shuddered, trying to breathe again.

"Lift her up. Get her out of there!" Dalton yelled.

"No, I've almost got it!"

The net cut free and the baby started to roll out, but her pectoral fin got caught. I reached down into the water and shook it. She tugged against it, trying to get free, making it worse.

I yanked the net, slipping it around her fin. She arched her back, flipped her tail, and she was free. With her weight gone, the harness shifted. I couldn't stop it. I plunged into the sea.

My muscles seized. I gasped, my body jerking with the reflex. Frigid water entered my lungs. Which way was up? *Ice. Cold. Darkness.* Something rammed me, bubbles everywhere. I burst to the surface, gasping for air, water coming out of my nose, my lungs on fire.

I reached for the harness, but grasped nothing but air. All

was a blur, a blue blur, my eyes smacked with icy pain. There was nowhere, nothing. I sucked in, coughed. My breath gone. My lungs frozen still.

The water churned around me and I was under again, immersed in searing numbness, pressing in on me from all directions. *Blackness*. My arms wouldn't move, my legs felt gone. Air? Where? I had to break from this icy grip.

My body wouldn't respond. Too...cold. Sinking. Sinking. No! I wriggled, moved. Dalton!

Waves pushing me away, away from the boat. Too late. Too far. Gone.

Then something pushed, raising me from the depths. Whoosh. I burst into the air. Free.

Hands, grabbing, pulling me from the sea.

Dalton's hands.

CHAPTER 22

I couldn't stop shivering. My hands were numb and I couldn't feel my feet. Dalton wrapped his wool blanket around both of us and pressed me against him, trying to get me warm. "Good thing Dylan was quick on the crane. The whales were going after you."

"No, no," I said, my teeth chattering. "They were pushing me up." *Weren't they? Yes.* "They were trying to save me."

He put his hand on my forehead. "No, I got you out before they really realized—"

"No, I…I know," I said. *I felt it. They knew I meant no harm. They knew.*

"Well, you're all right now," he said, hugging me tighter.

"Good thing you weren't in there any longer. You're in danger of hypothermia as it is," Bjørn said. "Let's get you inside." He shooed us toward the door like sheep. "All of you."

April, Dalton, and I were ushered into the galley.

"No hot coffee. Warm some milk," he said to Dylan who rushed around the tiny galley, opening and closing cupboard doors. "Just lukewarm. And maybe some oatmeal."

Dylan found a saucepan, but Bjørn snatched it from his hand. "I'll get it. Run down below and get her some dry clothes."

Dylan shook his head, his face turning pink, as though poking around in my suitcase was a trespass he wouldn't commit.

"It's all right," I said. "Grab anything. I don't mind."

His eyes fluttered about before he disappeared down the ladder.

Dalton and I settled onto the bench next to the heater.

"Not long now," Bjørn said. "I called Kystvakt. They're on the way."

"What?" I asked, my mind in a fog.

"The Norwegian Coast Guard," Dalton said. He had his arm around me, rubbing my other arm, trying to get me warm. "To take those three into custody."

I tried to massage my throbbing temples, but my hands were still cramped up and numb. "The cold water must have froze my brain."

Bjørn plopped a cup of warm milk on the table in front of me. "There. That'll help you thaw."

I looked to Dalton. "But I know. They were trying to save me."

"All right," he said, smiling.

Dylan appeared with an armful of clothes. He dropped them into a pile on the bench, then stood staring, his hands shoved in his pockets, not knowing what to do next.

Dalton rose from the bench and handed him a corner of the blanket. "Hold this up," he said. "Give her some privacy while she gets changed."

I reached for a sweatshirt but my hand still wouldn't grip. "I don't know if I can."

Dalton handed me the sweatshirt, worry etched on his face. "You have to get out of those wet clothes."

"I'll help her," April said and she started yanking at my pant legs, then pulled my shirt up over my head. I felt like an oversized toddler. She gave me a sympathetic frown. "Undies, too, don't you think? You want to be all cozy and dry."

Dylan cleared his throat and shuffled his feet. The blanket billowed with the movement.

I nodded and shifted on the bench, hooked my thumb into the waistband of my panties and slid them off. She unhooked my bra for me. I'd never been overly modest, but somehow being undressed by Dalton's new girlfriend was too much.

"I've got it. I've got it," I heard myself saying.

"Sorry," she said, barely a whisper.

"I didn't mean…" I frowned. "Thank you."

She nodded in understanding, then bunched up the sweatshirt and pulled it down over my head. I poked my arms through and she snugged it down. She did the same with my sweatpants, yanking them up my damp legs, then stepped back. "All right guys, she's dressed," she said.

Dalton ripped the blanket from Dylan's hand and wrapped it around me so snugly it felt like a baby's swaddle.

He leaned me against his chest and rubbed my arms. "How's that?" he said. "Feeling better? Is the feeling coming back to your hands? Let me see them."

"You've got me wrapped up too tight."

He flushed, embarrassed, and loosened the blanket.

I held out my left hand and he took it between his and held it, gently rubbing.

April watched with a curious expression. "I guess I owe you an apology," she said.

Dalton and I glanced at each other. We weren't sure which one of us she was talking to.

"Whatever for?" I asked.

She blushed. "I didn't realize you were a couple."

I sat back, yanking my hand from Dalton's grasp. "Oh, we're not," I said, shaking my head.

"Yeah…right," said Dalton, his hands finding the tops of his thighs and clamping on. "We're partners, that's all."

April looked from me to Dalton and back, then turned to Bjørn who was setting a bowl of oatmeal on the table. He grinned and gave her a wink.

"No, really," I said.

She gave us a mollifying smile. "Well, you make a good team."

I shook my head. Not me. I'd been stubborn and impulsive and put her and Dalton in danger. I got lucky I didn't end up fish food. I'd underestimated Ray. I had every intention of bluffing him, but he'd have shot me on the spot and dumped my body overboard.

I looked down at my bracelet and gave it a twist.

"Your dad would be proud of you," said Dalton.

My eyes clamped onto his. "Why would you say that?"

He shrugged. "You've been thinking about him all week. And today is…"

Something in his expression gave him away, a fleeting sign of guilt, then it was gone.

"You pulled his file," I said. An accusation.

"I was curious, is all," he said, all innocent. "I didn't think it would bother you."

I glared at him. What business was it of his what had happened to my dad? "Well, it does."

Dalton turned away, saying nothing. The silence lingered. I glanced around the galley. Dylan wiped at the counter with no particular purpose. Bjørn examined his thumbnail and April suddenly found her shirtsleeve interesting.

My stomach clenched. I hated making people feel uncomfortable.

"I'll go make our calls," said Dalton and rose from the bench.

"I'll 'elp wi' de radio," said Dylan, scurrying after him.

April's eyes flicked to the window, then the door as it shut. "I need the ladies' room," she said with an uncomfortable smile, then escaped to the head.

Bjørn stared at me with a fatherly expression. "Touchy subject, eh?"

I frowned and stared into my bowl of oatmeal.

He set his mug of coffee on the table and eased onto the bench across from me. "He cares about you, that boy. Good heart."

"He's my boss. I mean, my partner." I pushed a spoonful of oatmeal around in the bowl. "Whatever."

"Don't matter," he said. "The heart wants what the heart wants."

I said nothing. What could I say? And what the hell did he know about it anyway?

"I did know," he said. "What Ray was up to."

I raised my eyes to meet his.

"At first, I thought it was a fool's errand. And…" He stared into his coffee, then glanced around the galley, his eyes misty. "Well, I needed the money. This old boat…" He shook his head. "I had no idea he actually knew what he was doing. The other boats, the plane." He shook his head again. "I underestimated him."

Me too, I wanted to say. "Did you know about Svein?"

He rubbed his eyes and shook his head

"You helped me stop him. That's what I'm going to tell the authorities."

He examined me for a long moment with those sharp blue eyes, then gave me the slightest nod. "The Valkyrie," he said, almost a whisper. "She decides who lives and who dies."

"No," I said. "I believe, in the end, people get what they deserve."

The door to the head popped open and April came out. She hesitated. I smiled and she moved toward us and sat down. Dalton and Dylan tromped down the stairs and came back in.

"I've confirmed, the authorities are en route. Ten minutes out. And I called Joe. You're not going to believe what he said." He paused. "He wants us in Alaska."

"Are you serious?"

"You up for it?"

"Of course I'm up for it." I crossed my arms, suddenly feeling unsure. "But do you want me?"

The edge of his lip curved upward, ever so slightly. "Do you promise to stay out of the bars?"

"Funny," I said. "What's our directive in—oh, my video—" I pushed from the bench "—we'd better make sure—"

"Hold on," said Dalton, his hand on my arm. "You're still recovering."

I brushed past him. "I want to be sure we've got 'em," I said, heading for the crow's nest.

"Poppy!" He was right behind me.

I took the stairs two at a time, then started up the pole.

"You could get dizzy. Let me get it." He was right behind me.

"I'm fine."

"Both hands. Hang on with both hands," he was saying as he followed me up the pole, ready to catch me if I fell.

I climbed right up, unclipped the camera with one hand, and crawled into the bucket.

"Are you crazy? Do you know how high up we are?" Dalton said as he flipped a leg over and squeezed into the bucket with me.

"There's not exactly room for two," I said.

"Just check the video," he grumbled.

I clicked through the menu and hit play. The tiny monitor showed a perfect angle on the deck. I hit fast forward and there it was, like a Hollywood box office hit, in full Technicolor, Ray and Michael hauling baby Kimmy out of the water and onto the deck.

I grinned at Dalton. "We got 'em."

"We got 'em," he said with a nod, holding my gaze.

For the longest moment, I stared into his eyes. "Listen, I'm…" I had to look away.

"We got 'em," he said again.

"Yeah, but…" I swallowed and turned back to face him. "I underestimated them. I put you and April in danger and—" I sucked in my breath. "I never should have asked you to—"

"I don't do anything I don't want to do."

"Yeah, but I need to be more—"

"Poppy, there are bad guys in the world. There always will be." He smiled at me. His tummy-tingling smile. "Don't ever let it change who you are."

Yep. My tummy tingled.

"And look at that," he said, pointing over my shoulder. I spun around. A killer whale breached with a big splash.

"I thought they'd be long gone."

"Look!" April shouted from the deck below.

The mother whale was splashing and twirling in the water. The baby frolicked on the crest of her wake.

April held her hands over her mouth. "You did it. You saved her. You saved baby Kimmy!"

Dalton put his arm around my shoulders and whispered in my ear, "We do make a good team."

This guy, I swear.

Thank YOU for reading. If you would, PLEASE take a moment to post a review on <u>Amazon.com</u> or <u>Goodreads.com</u>. I would be grateful.

Author's Note

According to WDC, Whale and Dolphin Conservation, as of June 2015, in 14 marine parks in 8 different countries, there are:
- 56 orcas currently held in captivity (21 wild-captured plus 35 captive-born).
- 148 orcas have been taken into captivity from the wild since 1961.
- 161 orcas have died in captivity, not including 30 miscarried or still-born calves.

All for entertainment.

In 2013, seven wild orcas were captured by Russian fishermen in the Sea of Okhotsk for the mega-aquarium industry, the first caught in more than a decade. This is not a thing of the past.

Don't let the ads fool you. For every $1,000,000 SeaWorld makes, about $600 goes to conservation. That's 5 cents per ticket.

Please do NOT support them or any other marine park.

If you'd like to learn more and stay informed, please follow my blog at www.KimberliBindschatel.com or Poppy's rants on Facebook at www.Facebook.com/PoppyMcVie.

THANK YOU

This is my second novel in six months. I have no idea how I pulled that off other than with a lot of help and support.

Special thanks, again, to Professor David Favre of the Animal Law Center at MSU for all the advice and guidance. Any error is mine alone.

Many thanks to Lieutenant Jon Ardan of the U.S. Coast Guard for the details, but, more importantly, for dedicating his life to saving others from harm.

To Rachel and Dan for the painstaking rereads. It has made all the difference.

I am so thankful for my early readers—April, Diane, Tricia, Linda, Kathleen, Laura, Barbara, Andrea, Olivia, Erin, Ellen, and Jan. Their feedback was not only helpful, but encouraging.

Thanks also to April Parker for the inspiration for her namesake and for being a fan. Thanks to Scott Blair for helping with the sailing scene. I sail, but he's a true sailor.

As always, a special thank you to my loving and supportive husband. For some silly reason, he loves Poppy as much as he loves me. And to my parents, for raising me with a deep love of animals.

Thank YOU for reading. Please take a moment to post a review on Amazon.com or Goodreads.com I would be grateful.

ABOUT THE AUTHOR

Born and raised in Michigan, I spent summers at the lake, swimming, catching frogs, and chasing fireflies, winters building things out of cardboard and construction paper, writing stories, and dreaming of faraway places. Since I didn't make honors English in high school, I thought I couldn't write. So I started hanging out in the art room. The day I borrowed a camera, my love affair with photography began. Long before the birth of the pixel, I was exposing real silver halides to light and marveling at the magic of an image appearing on paper under a red light.

After college, I freelanced in commercial photography studios. During the long days of rigging strobes, stories skipped through my mind. As happens in life though, I was possessed by another dream—to be a wildlife photographer. I trekked through the woods to find loons, grizzly bears, whales, and moose. Then, for six years, I put my heart and soul into publishing a nature magazine, *Whisper in the Woods*. But it was not meant to be my magnum opus. This time, my attention was drawn skyward. I'd always been fascinated by the aurora borealis, shimmering in the night sky, but now my focus went beyond, to the cosmos, to wonder about our place in the universe.

In the spring of 2010, I sat down at the computer, started typing words, and breathed life into a curious boy named

Kiran in *The Path to the Sun*. Together, in our quest for truth, Kiran and I have explored the mind and spirit. Our journey has taken us to places of new perspective. Alas, the answers always seem just beyond our grasp, as elusive as a firefly on a warm autumn night.

Most recently, my focus has shifted to more pressing issues—imperiled wildlife. With the Poppy McVie series, I hope to bring some light into the shadowy underworld of black market wildlife trade, where millions of wild animals are captured or slaughtered annually to fund organized crime.

IT. MUST. STOP.

If you'd like to learn more and stay in touch, please sign up for my newsletter or follow my blog at www.KimberliBindschatel.com

The adventure doesn't end for Poppy and Dalton

Join them in Alaska as they pursue a grizzly bear poacher in

Order it today on

89755255R00122

Made in the USA
San Bernardino, CA
30 September 2018